THE MUSIC BOX

A NOVEL

Matt Micros

"Without music, life would be a mistake."
Friedrich Nietzsche

ISBN-10: 0996252614

ISBN-13: 978-0-9962526-1-4

TABLE OF CONTENTS

THE MUSIC BOX

For my father—the best man I ever knew

I
JOSH ~

*J*osh Reynolds had a perpetual smile on his face, even when he was nervous—which he was at that very moment. He was mid-to-late 30-something, but looked much younger than his age. Nearly always dressed in a pressed, blue Oxford and khakis, on this day, his shirt was unbuttoned at the top and the sleeves were folded up twice on each side. A tie hung loosely around his neck. That was Saturday casual dress at the biggest advertising agency in the world. He hated working weekends like most people hated the dentist, but deadlines were deadlines, and clients didn't differentiate between weekdays and weekends.

He checked his watch as he stepped into the elevator, before he realized he was stepping in front of a woman. He stopped, placed his arm in front of the doors, and waited for her to enter. She smiled at him the way all women did. Didn't matter who they were, women were drawn to his manners, easy charm and clean-cut good looks. They were gifts from his father without him even realizing it.

The door opened on the 2nd floor and a

disheveled looking man in his mid-20's stepped on. He looked as though he had been up most of the night. It was all he could do to nod at Josh in acknowledgment.

"Morning, Petey," Josh said. "You ready for the big presentation?"

"I think so," Pete answered with somewhat less confidence than Josh was hoping for.

"Well, let's hear it."

Pete paused, then motioned with his hands as if he was creating a billboard. "Why buy just one, when it might take five to do the trick?"

Josh stared at him in disbelief, his jaw dropping to almost floor level. "You're joking, right?"

"I don't think so," he said sheepishly.

"Petey, we're selling feminine protection here, not breath mints!"

"Well, we thought about going the other way. *Why buy a whole box, when one might do the trick?* But we thought the client might think we were encouraging people to buy less of their product."

"Good thinking," Josh said sarcastically. "Look, your saying will get people thinking about women who have..."

Pete looked puzzled. "Who have what?"

"Who have a heavy...you know."

"Heavy--"

The woman, silent until this point, leaned in. "Flow," she whispered.

"Thank you," Josh nodded before turning back to Pete. "Petey, we need to fix this or Bill's going to have a shit right there in the conference room.

I'm going to go stall him. You and Jimbo need to come up with an alternate slogan. And you need to do it fast, because my son's basketball game starts in two hours out in Connecticut."

"I think it might be a little late for that."

"Why??"

"Because Bill sent someone down to pick it up earlier this morning, so he could have an advance look at it."

"And you gave it to him??!!"

"He's my boss," Pete explained.

"I'M your boss!"

"But he's your boss."

"Which is why you should let me deal with him! This is not good. Bill's going to toss us all out of the 11th floor conference room window."

The elevator doors opened, and Josh raced down the hall to Bill Palmer's office. As he approached it, he could already hear Bill yelling from inside.

"Find Josh Reynolds!" Bill screamed at his secretary.

Josh motioned to her to pretend she hadn't seen him and did an abrupt 180 degree turn in the hallway. She just smiled at him. The way all women did.

Five minutes later, Josh slid into a seat next to Pete and Jim in the back of the conference room. There were ten other executives also in attendance. This would not be a pleasant experience he concluded.

"Did he look at the ad?" Pete asked nervously.

"I think it's safe to say that he did."

"Did he like it?"

"Let's just say, I hope your resume is up to date."

Bill entered the room. He was in his early 50's, with a thick head of mostly dark hair, with some grey sprinkled in. He had started as a copywriter twenty-seven years ago and worked his way up to CEO, stopping for a brief time at every rung of the ladder along the way. He was loud, bombastic even, but it was difficult not to respect a man who had actually worked his way to the top instead of having it handed to him.

"Josh," Bill began surprisingly calmly.

"Yes, Bill."

"What are my feelings on hiring morons?"

"You're generally opposed to it," Josh responded matter-of-factly, as if he was stating company policy.

"Exactly. It makes for bad business."

"That makes sense."

"Glad you agree with me. Now explain to me then, knowing how I feel about this, why you would put two morons in charge of one of our most lucrative clients?"

"Poor judgment on my part?" Josh offered, sending a steely look Pete and Jim's way.

"And what do they call the person who hired the two morons?" Bill continued.

"A bigger moron?"

"Exactly. *Why buy one when it might take five to do the trick?* Jesus H, we're not selling Hot Tamales here!"

Josh looked back at Pete as if to say he told

him so.

"What's the single most important factor to consider when selling feminine products?" Bill asked. "Jean?"

Jean was in her late 40's, most likely past her tampon usage days. Her eyes grew wide. She wasn't expecting to have to answer any questions. She preferred to work behind the scenes and be neither praised nor yelled at.

"Comfort?" she responded shyly.

"Good. And what else? Josh?"

"Uh, I've never used one, Bill."

"Neither have I," he answered, not missing a beat. "But I've seen them in trashcans. I'm sure you have too. And what's your reaction when you stumble onto one?"

"Eww?"

"Exactly. And what is one of the primary advantages our product offers?"

"Discretion?"

"Bullseye. So let's sell some goddamn discretion then! What I need is for you and the other two morons to sit here until you figure this shit out. Tell your wives you won't be home until you've got a slogan we can pitch. I've got to go see my chiropractor. Text me when you're done."

Josh rose from his seat. He knew it was a poor time to make a stand, but decided to make it anyway. "Bill," he said as he checked his watch, "I've actually got to leave for a while. My son's league championship basketball game starts in forty-five minutes out in Connecticut."

"And I'm sure it will be a helluva game. But

he's ten."

"12 actually."

"Fine. He's 12. But don't act like it's the NBA Finals. Take care of this, Josh, because the only thing worse than being the guy who hired two morons is being the guy who hired the moron who hired two morons. Because you know what that makes him?"

"The biggest moron?"

"Exactly. And I have no intention of being the biggest moron."

"I hear ya, Bill. But I still have to leave."

There was a palatable uncomfortableness in the room.

"I wouldn't if you value your job."

"I do. Value my job that is. But I value my son even more. I'll make sure I'm reachable and will stay up all night if I need to, in order to make this right," Josh said as he made his way toward the door, leaving a stunned Bill in his wake. He decided not to look back because he knew if he did, he might start to have second thoughts.

~

Josh made what was usually a 50 minute drive in 39 minutes and slid into a seat in the bleachers next to a pretty blonde woman a few years younger than him.

Colleen Reynolds was the soccer mom who brought the oranges at halftime of games. The mother that all teenage boys eventually got teased about because she was so attractive. The wife that made Josh the envy of all his friends, and even a few enemies. Colleen was a sweetheart, but like all good mothers, someone who was fiercely protective of her son.

"Didn't think you were going to make it," she said.

"Yeah, I had to walk out in the middle of a meeting and drive 120 miles an hour on the Merritt in order *to* get here, but I wouldn't have missed it."

"He's been looking into the stands every couple of minutes for you."

Almost on cue, Timmy Reynolds looked up, broke into a wide smile and waved to his father. It suddenly made the nerve-wracking drive and his job uncertainty completely worthwhile.

"Little boys and their fathers," Colleen smiled. "He lights up every time you walk into a room."

"Give it a couple of years and he'll be giving me the finger and telling me I'm an a-hole," Josh answered. "By the way, I hope you're well-stocked in feminine products, because I don't think we're going to be getting any more free samples any time soon."

Thirty-two text messages and four phone calls from Pete later, and they finally had a new slogan. He missed a few minutes of the game, but at least he was there. Later that night, he entered his son's dimly lit room to tuck him in and sat down on one corner of the bed.

"Night, pal," Josh said. "You played a great game today."

"Thanks for comin, dad," Timmy answered, before adding what was really on his mind. "You're not going to get fired, are you?"

18

"Of course not. Why do you ask?"

"Because mom said you left an important meeting to come to my game."

"I'll be ok. Besides, like my dad used to say, 'Family first, last, and in between,'" Josh said as he stood in the doorway. "Night, pal."

"What was he like?" Timmy asked.

"What was who like? My dad?" Josh responded, a bit surprised by the question.

It was something that had been on Timmy's mind for a while. His grandfather had passed away before he had been born, but since his dad rarely spoke of him, he hadn't before mustered the courage to ask.

"Yeah."

"He was..." Josh reflected, "Complicated. But he was a good man."

Josh nodded. He seemed pleased with himself that he had found the right word to describe him.

"Did he used to go to your games?"

"Yes. But I didn't know it at the time."

"How come?"

"It's kind of a long story, pal."

"I'm not very tired," Timmy reasoned.

Josh mulled it over. Decided there was no time like the present. After a slight pause, he began, "My dad.....was smart. He was athletic. Funny. Charming. Beautiful women fell all over him."

"How do you know that?"

"He got your grandmother to marry him, didn't he?"

"No offense, dad, but grandma's old—and wrinkly."

Josh chuckled, "Well, she wasn't always. When your grandmother was younger, everyone thought she was gorgeous."

"Tell me more about your dad," Timmy urged.

"I'll tell you about him on two conditions. One. You keep it between you and I. Not even your mother or grandmother know some of the things I'm about to tell you. And two. If your mother walks in, you shut your eyes and pretend to be asleep so she doesn't yell at me for keeping you up past your bedtime. Deal?"

"Deal," Timmy assured him as he sat up in bed waiting for the story to begin.

"Ok, then. It was my 12th birthday...."

II
THE MUSIC BOX~1991

*T*immy Reynold's grandmother was as pretty as Josh had described her to his son, in a 1990's sort of way. She had waves of neatly arranged blonde hair, deeply expressive green eyes, and a backside whose superiority was barely concealed by the pair of form fitting tan pants she was wearing. A single mom at a time where she was in the minority, Jane was extremely involved in her only son's life. She was the Head of the PTA. She ran the school bake sales. And she was the soccer mom that drove multiple kids to the games and brought orange slices for halftime. Other mothers looked at her with equal parts adulation, fear and resentment. Adulation for her many talents. Fear for the same exact reason. And resentment because she forced them to keep the nagging of their husbands to a minimum, lest any of them decide to up and leave them for her. The fact that she would never have done that to any of them still didn't make them feel much better about it.

She had just tossed the last of a stack of thick pancakes onto a pile that could have fed four people, but she had made for two, when the doorbell rang. On the other side of it was her sister. Five years her senior, one glance was all it took to recognize that Cheryl and her were related, with many of the same pretty, delicate features. Cheryl just had a few more rings around the oak tree; a little more wear on the tires.

"To what do I owe this early morning pleasure? Are you hungry? I just finished making some pancakes. Josh will never eat them all," Jane said casually.

"No thanks," Cheryl responded as she walked inside. She clearly had something on her mind. "Nick has taken a very bad turn," she continued. "He's back home. But it's a matter of time. I thought you'd want to know."

Jane had always owned the ability to mask what she was really feeling at any given moment. It was as much a defense mechanism as anything. "I'm sorry to hear that," she said at last.

"He's asking to see you and Josh," Cheryl blurted out as if she was ripping off a band-aid. Telling Jane something she didn't want to hear was a bit like stepping in front of a moving bus. You knew it was going to hurt. You just hoped you survived.

"That's not going to happen."

"I think it's time to let it go. If not for yourself, then for Josh."

"He's barely been a part of Josh's life in five years. I don't mean to sound callous, but I don't think the week he's dying is the time to start."

"He hasn't been a part of his life because you have shielded Josh from him."

"Because I didn't want him to break his heart anymore than he already has," Jane reasoned.

"Are you sure you're talking about Josh? Jane, he didn't cheat on you. He just made some poor decisions."

"Whose side are you on? You're supposed to be my sister."

"I am your sister. But I'm also his friend. I'm the one who introduced you two, remember?"

"Of course I remember. And yes, I know he's not a bad guy. It's just too difficult to be around him."

"Whatever you decide for yourself is obviously up to you, but I don't think you should make that decision for Josh. You won't get a second chance," Cheryl added for emphasis. "We're talking a matter of days here."

"I wanna see him," said a voice from the open doorway on the other side of the room. Josh at twelve looked like a shrunken down version of himself at 37. Tight, directionless waves of light brown hair with eyes that matched his mother's.

There wasn't much Jane could say to that.

"Are you sure, honey?"

"It's my birthday."

"I know it is."

"You said I could do whatever I wanted."

"And that's where you want to go?"

"Yes."

"Ok then," she said with a forced smile.

Josh spent the better part of the remainder of the morning locked in his room, with the faintest strains of music willowing out from beneath the crack at the bottom of his door. As his mother drew closer to the room, she could make out The Beatles, "*In My Life*" playing out of a double deck tape recorder.

"Whatcha doin?" she asked as she poked her head into the room.

"Just making a mix tape of songs dad likes. I'm almost done," Josh answered.

Jane seemed visibly surprised. "How do you know what music he likes?"

"Because he talked about them in the letters he sent me. Asked me to listen to them. Said they'd—"

She finished his sentence for him with a smile.

"—change your life."

"How'd you know?"

"I used to be married to him. Let me guess. Frank Sinatra?"

"Yes."

"Nick Drake?"

"Yup."

"What else?"

"James Taylor."

"Which song?"

"Something in the Way She Moves. You know it?"

A sad expression overtook her face. "Yes, I know it. You almost ready to go?"

"Can we stop at once place first?"

They had been driving for about ten minutes before Josh pointed to the neon sign that read,

"Big Al's". It was a somewhat dingy storefront on the outskirts of downtown. Stamford was an interesting city. On one side, it was typical Fairfield County, Connecticut with beachfront homes, Range Rovers, Mercedes and pristinely kept yards. On the other side of the tracks, if you will, were storefronts with bars on the windows, automotive repair shops and sidewalks in need of repair. Big Al's was on that side of town.

"That's the place," Josh said.

"That's where you want to go??" his shocked mother responded.

"I go there all the time. They have something I want to buy."

"Lovely. My twelve year old son hangs out in pawn shops," she said dryly.

Al lived up to his name. He was large. Slightly unkempt. In need of a shower. And a possessor of a somewhat surly demeanor. It wouldn't be a stretch to picture him smashing someone in the face with his bare fist or hoisting them against the wall of his establishment just for looking at him the wrong way. And yet, he seemed to have a soft spot for Josh.

"Haven't seen you in a while. You browsing or buying today?" Al asked.

"Buying," Josh answered confidently.

Josh guided his mother through the cluttered rows of jackets, jewelry, pocket-knives, books and golf clubs to where the radios and stereos were. She was careful not to brush up against anything while she walked. Jane didn't want to offend, but more than that, she didn't want to take the chance of picking up any potential airborne illnesses that might be associated with nearly every item in the store.

Josh pointed to a small wooden music box with a white ivory top trimmed in cherry oak. It was surprisingly beautifully crafted with an ornate design surrounding the interlocking emblem "ND" of the University of Notre Dame painted onto the ivory. Inside, instead of the normal mechanisms usually found inside a music box, was a tape deck. It was a case of old meeting new.

"That's it," he pointed.

"It's forty dollars," his mother said.

"That your girlfriend?" Big Al said to Josh with a smile.

His mother wasn't amused.

"My mother," Josh answered with a roll of his eyes.

Al nodded indicating he felt his pain.

Turning to his mother Josh said, "I've got twenty dollars saved up from my allowance. Besides, you said I could pick out something I wanted for my birthday."

"I was thinking more along the lines of a Jets jersey or jacket. Not a wooden box from a pawn shop." She quickly turned to Al. "No offense."

"None taken. Tell you what. Normally 40. I'll sell it to you for twenty-five. Happy Birthday."

How could she say no now?

"But you already have a tape player."

"It's not for me," Josh said.

"The idea of your birthday is that you're supposed to get something for yourself."

"Not this year," he said determinedly.

He pulled out twenty dollars in fives and ones and placed the bills on the counter.

"Put your money away. I've got it," she said.

"I'll even throw in a box and a ribbon," Al offered.

A pawn shop owner with a heart.

Once in the car—Josh never counted his money in the open street--he counted the change that his mother had let him keep. He furrowed his brow when he realized it was too much.

"We have to go back," he said quickly.

"What? Why?"

"Because he gave us too much change. It was twenty-five dollars and we gave him thirty. There's ten dollars here."

"Are you sure?"

Josh held up two fives.

"We have to go back," he repeated.

"Ok. Ok. We'll go back," she said as she made a U-Turn.

Josh walked back into the store and handed Big Al the extra five.

"What's this?" Al asked.

"You gave us too much change. It should have only been five," Josh explained.

"Well, this has to be a first," Al laughed heartily. "Tell you what. You keep it just for being honest."

His mother smiled in the background. Even she had started to warm up to Big Al.

III
NO HONOR WITHOUT HONESTY~

*I*t took all of five minutes in a room with Nick Reynolds to wonder how anyone could ever think poorly of him. He was handsome, charming, funny and had that disarming ability to make you feel as though you were among his most intimate friends after a few short moments. People were drawn to him. Most guys wanted to *be* him. Everyone else wanted to at least be *around* him, because when they were, life was that much better.

And yet, to those that knew him best, he was an enigma. While he was outgoing to strangers, family and friends alike, he only allowed people to get so close before slamming the door shut on his life. He wasn't a bad person. He was just guarded. Exactly why this was so, was a mystery to all.

He lived by himself in a mansion just off Main Street in the wealthiest town in the wealthiest county in Connecticut. The house said a lot about the man. It was a rebuilt colonial with grey vinyl, shake shingle siding and white trim. The shake shingle showed his love of all things old, but the fact that it was vinyl instead of wood, was because he valued ease of maintenance even more. On the roof was a widow's walk, from which he could look out at the Long Island Sound on one side, and the center of town on another. It signified someone you could see, but might have a difficult time reaching. Surrounding the house on all sides was a man-built stone wall and wrought iron gate, that protected it from outsiders. The gate was more symbolic than anything, as he usually left it open. He just liked how it looked.

The yard was immaculately kept by his checkbook, rather than his own actual blood and sweat. When he first bought the house, he dreamed of weekends spent cutting the lawn and trimming the landscaping, but even the best-laid plans were subject to reality. There were only so many hours in a week.

Jane drove past the gate and pulled in front of the house in her Mercedes E Class sedan. She seemed hesitant to get out of the car, but Josh climbed out immediately and walked so purposefully toward the door that his mother had little choice but to follow. He rang the doorbell with a firm push of the button.

His uncle answered the door and hugged them both. Dan Reynolds was the younger brother of Josh's dad by five years. He was more flannel shirt than Armani suit, with the straightforward, easy demeanor of the high school gym teacher that he was.

"I'm glad you came," Dan said. "He'll be thrilled. Just to warn you, he's in kind of tough shape."

The house had always reminded Josh of the White House tour his mother had taken him on a couple of years back. Ornate molding. A grand staircase that led to a baluster overlook. Expensive throw rugs and cherry oak bookcases. It was so neatly arranged and clean that it was difficult to even picture someone actually living there. They walked down the corridor to a room at the end of the hall. Dan opened the door and held it open for them.

"You go ahead," his mother told him. "Have a little alone time with your father. I'll visit with Dan for a bit first."

Josh entered and closed the door behind him. He was a little more hesitant after actually seeing his father. He was sitting up in bed, and it appeared as though it was taking every ounce of energy to do even that. However, even in his fragile state, Nick Reynolds was still a commanding presence. Handsome, well-chiseled features. Deep, soulful blue eyes. He lit up at the sight of his son and seemed to sit up a little taller.

"Hey, pal. Wow, you've gotten tall. How have you been?"

"I'm ok," Josh answered quietly.

"What have you been doing with yourself?"

"Basketball ended a few weeks ago."

"And you guys won the championship!" his father exclaimed.

"How did you know that?"

Josh was a little tentative around him. He had wanted to see him, but he hadn't spent much time with him in the last five years.

"Because Reynolds men always win. That, and the fact that I was there."

"You were there?!"

"Wouldn't have missed it. You're a better ball handler than I ever was."

"Why didn't you tell me you were coming?"

"Well, I wasn't sure if I was going to make it, and I've learned over the years to not promise something I wasn't sure I could deliver. And then once I got there, you seemed pretty busy, so I didn't want to distract you."

"It wouldn't have been a distraction. I would have introduced you to my friends and coaches."

The only inkling that Nick felt guilty was that he quickly changed the subject. "So what else is going on? Any girls in your life?"

"Uh...no."

"Why not?" his father asked. "Reynolds men have always been popular with the ladies. I had my first girlfriend when I was ten!"

Josh had skated with a couple of girls at roller skating parties, but that was about the extent of his pre-pubescent love life.

"I brought something for you," Josh said at last.

He placed the wrapped box with a ribbon on top next to his father on the bed.

"It's your birthday and you're giving *me* presents?" Nick exclaimed.

Nick opened it with a smile and slowly removed the music box. "It is....*without* question....the most beautiful thing I have ever seen."

Josh lifted the lid for him, revealing the tape deck inside. "I know you went to Notre Dame and it plays music."

He pulled out the cassette tape he made for his father and inserted it into the music box.

"What's on that?" Nick asked excitedly.

"It's a mix of songs I know you like."

"Frank Sinatra?" he winked at his son.

"Play it."

Nick pushed the button and after a second or two delay, Bruce Springsteen's "Thunder Road" began its piano introduction.

At first, the room seemed to *freeze*. And then it began to fade away as if the two of them had been transported back in time. But how could they have been?

Both father and son had the identical puzzled look on their faces as they observed younger versions of themselves together. Neither was sure whether it was really happening, or if the music had simply triggered the same memory in each other. It was impossible to tell the difference.

~

Nick was driving with seven year old Josh in the passenger seat. This was long before the days when seven year olds were required to sit in the back.

"We're going to be late," Josh moaned.

"No we won't. It's 4:20 now. We'll race to the hardware store, and I'll have you at Peter's house by 5 o'clock," his father answered.

"Why do we have to go to the hardware store now?"

"Because the lights are out on both the lamp post and front porch and I don't like the idea of your mother coming home in the dark."

"Haven't they been out for a while?"

"A few weeks. Doesn't mean I like it. Just means I've been busy."

Nick and Josh entered the small, family run business with a wave to the owner. Sam was a hard working, smart businessman, who had owned and operated the store for nearly fifty years. It had been there before Greenwich had become Greenwich and he saw no reason to relocate. After all, mansions needed light bulbs, shovels, paint, and nuts and bolts too. Even if the owners usually sent people who worked for them to purchase them. Nick was one of the few who did his own shopping and one of the few residents Sam knew by name.

"Hi Sam. Where are your light bulbs again?"

"Aisle 3. All the way to the back on the right. And how are you, young man?" he added when he saw Josh.

"Fine."

"Helping your father with his errands, huh?"

"Yes."

"Not very talkative today I see," Sam laughed.

Nick returned from the back with an armful of bulbs.

"He's late for a birthday party," he explained. "Or at least he thinks he will be."

"Well, then let's not waste time talking and get you rung up."

Sam punched in the price of each package into the cash register. There was no such thing as a scanner back then.

"That will be seven dollars and twenty-three

cents," Sam said.

Nick handed him a crisp ten-dollar bill. Sam placed it under the drawer, the way one would with a hundred dollar bill today and handed him his change. Nick gave it to his son.

"You keep track of the change," he said, and Josh knew that meant he would get to keep it.

The clock hands in the car read 5:20 and Josh fidgeted accordingly.

"Did you count the change?" Nick asked. "You should always count your change."

Josh glanced at it in his hands.

"Three dollars and seventy-seven cents," he anwered.

Nick looked puzzled. "How much?"

"Three-seventy-seven," Josh repeated.

"And how much did everything come to?"

"I don't remember," Josh lied. He just knew the discovery would further delay his arrival at the party.

"Check the receipt."

Josh glanced at it and confirmed what he already knew to be true, but didn't want to say anything, since they were already running late.

"What's it say?" Nick insisted.

"$7.23," Josh finally blurted out.

"So Sam gave us an extra dollar!" Nick exclaimed as if he had just discovered the Theory of Relativity. "We have to go back."

"Why? It's only a dollar."

"Because it's the right thing to do."

"Ok, but do we have to go back now? We're

already late. Can't we go back tomorrow?"

"No, we can't go back tomorrow. What if Sam runs out of change for his customers? What if he needs to pick something up on the way home and is a dollar short?"

"That's just dumb," Josh wailed.

"It's not dumb. It's called being honest," his father responded.

Nick walked back into the store a few minutes later, waved, then placed the dollar down on the counter, while several other customers looked on.

"You gave us an extra dollar's change, Sam."

"I'm sure I'll see you again. You didn't have to come all the way back here right now," Sam laughed.

"A dollar buys a lot of things. You never know when you'll need it." Nick wasn't grandstanding. He said it matter-of-factly and he truly believed what he was saying.

"Well, if I only make my mortgage payment by a dollar, I'll be sure and thank you."

"Gotta run. Son has a party to get to."

Everyone seemed flabbergasted that he would go to such trouble for one dollar.

"The world's first and last honest lawyer," Sam chuckled once Nick had left.

The fifteen-minute drive felt like an hour to Nick, the way it always did when you were late and had an upset seven year old pouting in the passenger seat. Nick glanced at his watch after ringing the doorbell. He seemed a little embarrassed that they were so late. It was nearly 6:00 now. Josh's friend's mother seemed surprised at the late arrival, but did her best to make Josh feel welcome.

"My apologies for being so late, Betty," Nick said.

"Come in. Come in. I'm really sorry. We didn't think Josh was going to make it so we already cut the cake. But there are still a few kids playing out back. And I'll check to see if there's any cake left."

It may not have been the end of the world, but when seen through the eyes of a seven year old, it certainly seemed that way. Josh barely acknowledged his father as he walked past.

~

Back in Nick's bedroom in present day, Josh sat on the edge of the bed as the last sounds of *"Thunder Road"* faded into the background.

"I missed everything," Josh said.

"I wouldn't exactly call a piece of cake everything," his father replied. "Joshua, over the course of your life, between birthdays, weddings and parties, you'll probably eat a thousand pieces of cake. Literally a thousand. Missing one isn't a great tragedy. But missing a life lesson? Now, that would be."

"Life lesson?"

Mark Twain once said, "Always do the right thing. It will gratify some people, and astonish the rest." Besides, you can have no honor without honesty. *That* is your life lesson."

IV
THE AMMENDMENT ~

Nick Reynolds was OCD long before it was in vogue to be OCD. His coins need to be evenly and neatly stacked in small piles. His pens all needed to be facing the same direction and not touching each other. Magazines and coasters needed to be symmetrically spaced out on the coffee table. Trash cans could not be placed across any lines on tile or stone floors. And of course there were the lists. He began each day with a small notepad list of things he needed to take care of that day. Some were time consuming like trying a court case. Others were as simple as making the bed or showering, toweling off, shaving, and getting dressed. They counted as four.

As the day would go on, items would inevitably get added to the list and other things would take longer than expected, which meant there was rarely a day where he was able to complete everything. Which in turn meant he rarely had a relaxing night's sleep. He would lay awake for hours, his mind whirring at the list of things he had yet to accomplish.

As the first notes of Billy Joel's *"Captain Jack"*

escaped from the music box, Nick and his son's expressions indicated they had been transported back to one such day.

Saturdays always began with hand-washing the car. Keeping a car so clean you could literally eat off the dashboard if you needed to was a Reynold's men tradition. And of course there was a method involved.

"You have to wash the car from the top down," Nick told his son.

"Why?" Josh asked.

"Because if you don't, the soap will run over onto parts you've already washed."

"So?"

"So then you've got to rinse them again. Water isn't free, you know."

"It isn't?"

"*Nothing* in the world is free," Nick reiterated. "As your grandmother always says, *there's no such thing as a free lunch.*"

"I had a free lunch last week at the McKettrick's house," Josh answered.

"You thought it was free. But someday, they'll remind you of the ham sandwich they gave you and want something in return."

"They made me bologna."

"Well, then they'll remind you of the bologna sandwich," Nick laughed.

"I don't get it."

"You will someday. Don't forget to use the thick sponge before towel drying the car."

"What's the difference?"

"Because it absorbs the excess water so your towel doesn't get too wet and leave streaks all over, which then become water spots."

"That's dumb. Why can't we take our cars to the car wash like everyone else?"

"Because car washes scratch the paint on your car. The only people who take their cars to a car wash are people who don't care about their cars. And people who don't care about their cars are usually sloppy people that don't care about their appearance. They don't shower very often and they wear clothes with rips and tears in them. You don't want to be one of those people do you, Joshey?"

"I guess not."

"Make sure you turn off the hose," Nick said as he packed up the sponges and towels.

~

Nick, with Josh in tow, walked down a hospital corridor carrying several bags. Josh had a couple himself.

"Hello, Mrs. Butwin!" Nick exclaimed as he pulled a bouquet of fresh flowers from one of the bags. "Lovely day today."

Mrs. Butwin was in her mid-80's with failing health and didn't think any day was particularly lovely.

Nick pulled back the curtains. "Can I do anything for you?"

"Can you help me have a bowel movement? I haven't had one in days."

He was a bit caught off guard by the comment. "I could see if the nurses have any prune juice?

"Prune juice tastes like..."

"Prunes?" Nick offered.

"Shit," Mrs. Butwin responded.

"That's probably why it's so effective in helping you do just that," he reasoned with a smile.

It was part of Nick's charm. He had a way of disarming even the sourest of personalities.

"How's Bea?" she asked.

"She's good. She's had several bowel movements," he said with a wink. "And don't worry. I dropped off the groceries and unpacked them for her. She's all set."

"How much do we owe you?"

"You don't owe me anything."

"You can't keep buying us groceries. We have plenty of money."

"Save it for a rainy day."

"I'm 87 years old. I don't have that many days left, rainy or otherwise."

"Nonsense. You're going to outlive us all."

"God, I hope not," she grumbled.

"Who was that lady, dad?" Josh asked after they had left the room.

"Just a client of mine."

"I thought clients were supposed to pay you?"

"What do you mean?"

"You said you bought her groceries."

Nick smiled. "Her and her husband paid me quite a bit of money over the years and were quite good to me. Getting her and her daughter groceries is the least I can do."

"What happened to her husband?"

"He died a few years ago. And her daughter is struggling health wise."

"What's wrong with her?"

"She has a disease called MS. It makes it difficult for her to walk and get around."

"That's terrible. Does she need help with anything else? I could mow their lawn for them."

"I'm sure they'd appreciate that," Nick responded as he tussled with Josh's hair.

They took the elevator to another floor and Josh followed his dad past the nurse's station.

"Hi Nick," one of the nurses said with a flirtatious smile.

"Janice. Always a pleasure," Nick answered with mock formality as he knocked on the door to one of the rooms.

A man lay in an uncomfortable state in the bed, flipping through the television stations in search of something to distract him from the pain. Nick placed a box of cookies on a table by the window. The man in the bed motioned for him to hand them to him instead.

"Hey there, Josh," the man said, mustering up the courage to be friendly.

"How are you feeling, Mr. Flynn?"

"Terrible, but thank you for asking."

"Jane sends her best," Nick said.

"Did she send any naked pictures as well?"

"Afraid not," Nick chuckled. "Just the cookies."

"Love Jane's cookies. Love Jane. In fact, the entire neighborhood wonders how you managed to land her. You must be hung like Secretariat is all we can figure."

"I prefer to think it's my rugged good looks and dashing charm that wooed her."

"Be serious, Reynolds. Mussolini had more charm. But thanks for the cookies. I never realized how painful kidney stones could be."

"Any luck passing them?"

"I wouldn't call it *luck*. You try shoving a golf ball through a straw and let me know how that works out."

"I'm not sure chocolate chip cookies will help in that area much," Nick reasoned.

"Oh well. I'll suffer."

"When are they letting you out of here?"

"Probably tomorrow. They're giving me boiled asparagus with three cans of coke for lunch today."

"That sounds disgusting."

"Apparently, the combination of the two will help dissolve the stones."

"Who's your doctor? Some ancient tribal witch doctor?!"

"At this point, I'll try anything."

"Let me know how it goes."

"Just leave your window open at home and you'll hear the screams. You're only ten miles away."

"I'll see you later," Nick laughed. "Let me know if you need me to shag your wife for you."

"I'd *pay* you to do that."

"What does *shag* mean?" Josh asked once in the hallway. "And why would Mr. Flynn pay you to do that?"

"It means *visit*," Nick answered. "And because he doesn't want her to be lonely while he's in the hospital."

"Who are we visiting next?"

"Now, we get to see Uncle Dan."

"Uncle Dan is the best!"

"Yes he is."

When Dan couldn't find anything that looked appealing on the TV, he turned on a small radio beside his bed. *Captain Jack* was playing. Nick didn't knock before entering this room. He dropped the magazines and books down on the table.

"Sports Illustrated. Swimsuit Issue. Car and Driver. The Daily News. It's all about the Mets."

"Yeah, and I watched the pennant clinching game from a hospital bed."

"Don't get pneumonia next time."

"It wasn't something I was shooting for."

"You were outside in the rain with no jacket, hat, or umbrella for five hours straight."

"The weatherman said cloudy with a 10% chance of showers."

"Haven't you learned that they're never right? Maybe they will be someday when technology improves, but right now, you'd be better off asking Punxsutawney Phil for his opinion."

"So how was the game?"

"Not to make you feel worse, but guess who was in the suite next to us?"

"Billy Joel!" Josh screamed.

"Are you shitting me? Excuse my French,

Joshey."

"And he did an acapella version of *Captain Jack* for us."

"I suppose you're also going to tell me you met Gia Carangi as well? And drank for free? And had a limousine drive you home?"

"How'd you know?" Nick smirked.

"I hate you."

"Get out of the hospital then and we can catch a World Series game."

"They're sending me home on the weekend."

"I'll pick up tickets to game two at Shea. Can't promise that Billy Joel will sing to you though."

"I'll settle for a win."

"Can't promise that either, Dano."

Nick and Josh were walking toward their car when Nick looked up at a sign that read, "No Exit Without a Token". He then looked at the guard gate and saw no one inside. The token-change machine was "out-of-order". A sign on it read, "Go to hospital front desk for tokens."

Nick grudgingly walked back *into* the hospital he had just exited. A girl at the welcome desk was chatting away on the phone.

"Tokens for the parking lot?" Nick asked, trying not to disturb her too much.

She didn't break a sentence. Simply motioned with her arm for him to go down another corridor. At his 3rd desk, when he was convinced he had almost completed a rectangle, he finally had success.

Nick had buckled Josh in and was about to

climb into the driver's seat of his car, a 1968 cherry red, Mustang convertible, when he noticed another man walking towards his own car.

"Hope you've got a token!" Nick shouted.

"They don't have them out here?" the man asked.

"Nope. And the machine is broken. I had to walk about two miles and go to three different desks to get one."

"You didn't happen to get two, did you?" the man asked hopefully.

"It was hard enough to get one! But I tell you what. Pull your car up behind mine. I'll put in my token and when the gate goes up, I'll punch it. Get right on my tail and we'll both get through."

"You sure?"

"No problem. Serve these idiots right for not having someone out here working."

"Thanks. I appreciate it."

Nick pulled up to the gate with the man directly behind him. He inserted the token into the slot and hit the gas. There was only one problem. The gate hadn't gone up yet. He shattered it into a hundred pieces with wood splintering in every direction. The man pulled up next to him just outside the exit with eyes as wide as saucers. Police sirens began to wail in the not so far off distance.

"Sure. *Now* they come." Turning to the guy, he said, "You better get out of here. I'll take care of it."

"You sure?"

Nick spoke as if this was a regular occurrence.

"Yeah. No problem."

He didn't have to ask him twice. The man drove away as Hospital Security approached in a spiffy Ford Escort.

"What happened?!"

"Your gate's broken.

"It requires a token."

"Oh, I used a token. It took me about twenty minutes, two miles and three desks to get one, but I found one."

The guard checked the machine. Sure enough, he found a token inside.

"I told you."

"So what happened?"

"The gate started to go up and then as I was driving through, it came down again. Could have killed me. And it scratched the hell out of my car. Hope you guys have insurance."

"We'll take care of it," the guard assured him. "Let me have all your information. I'm really sorry about that."

"It's ok," Nick said. "But you might want to have someone out here monitoring things."

"I'll mention it to my supervisor."

Josh sat in silence as he watched security drive away.

"I thought you said to always be honest?" he said.

"That's true, with the exception being if you're trying to help someone, and telling the truth would end up costing you a lot of money," Nick explained.

~

"Is that Life Lesson #2?" Josh asked as he remained bedside next to his father.

"Actually it's really more like #1A."

Then Nick began laughing so hard he started to cough. Josh rushed to hand him a glass of water.

"Are you ok?" he asked.

Nick took a sip. "Thanks. Just makes me laugh thinking about that guy going home and telling his family about the lunatic who blasted through the gate to spring him out of the hospital. He probably thought I escaped from the Psych Ward."

"Probably," Josh joined him in laughter. "You smashed that gate to bits!"

"Anytime I hear *Captain Jack*, it reminds me of that day," Nick said almost wistfully.

"Me too."

Nick nodded, pleasantly surprised that the day seemed to mean something to his son as well. "I need to close my eyes for a few minutes, pal, but will you sit with me while I do?"

"Sure."

"Means a lot to me that you came by today. Wish I had the strength to take you somewhere fun for your birthday."

"It's ok, dad. Maybe when you're feeling better."

"Yeah," Nick nodded with a sad smile, "maybe when I'm feeling better."

V
ONCE IN A LIFETIME ~ 1979

*N*ick fastened his tie in a dimly lit room and leaned over to kiss his wife on the cheek. "Morning, babe. How are you feeling?"

Jane rolled onto her back revealing her large belly. "Like I can't wait to have this baby. Can't we ask the doctor to reach in and pull it out??"

"Afraid not, but you're getting close," he responded as he checked his watch. "I've got to run and catch my flight."

"Do you really have to go?"

"Afraid so."

"What if my water breaks?"

"Water can't break, babe. It's a liquid."

"Very funny, smart ass."

"You're not due for a couple of weeks yet, and I'll be home in two days," Nick reasoned. "If you need anything, Cheryl is next door, and I've left my hotel and office numbers on the kitchen table. I love you."

"Love you too."

He had 51 minutes to catch his flight and lived 35 minutes from the airport. Back in 1979, all bags flew free on all airlines, you could bring shampoo bottles and shaving cream cans in your carry on without worrying about their size, security didn't involve disrobing in front of complete strangers, and you could still make a flight if you arrived at the airport 11 minutes before departure.

Nick pleaded his case to one of the security guards, who pulled him from the line and escorted him through at a full sprint. He arrived at the gate just as the stewardess was about to close the door, but instead of making a snotty comment and refusing entry, she waved him on and he received a rousing ovation from the other passengers the way the last person on frequently did back then.

Six hours later, Nick's plane touched down at LAX. Driving a rental car in five lanes of traffic while trying to read a Thomas Guide to help him get to where he was going was not a task for the feint of heart. He was flipped off at least twice in the first ten minutes, then blocked from exiting where he wanted to go by someone who thought he was trying to be cheeky and avoid traffic.

"I now understand road rage," he muttered to himself. Eventually, he arrived at a two-story office building on Wilshire Boulevard in the heart of Beverly Hills. It was sparsely decorated on the inside, with people working on improving that aspect of it at that very moment. A handful of employees worked in the background of the oversized conference room where Nick met with two immaculately groomed young men. Both were seated on the same side of a large, oval deep oak table while Nick stood before them.

"Gentlemen. Our law firm is one of the oldest

and most respected firms in the country. But we also recognize that you have to stay ahead of the changing times, so we're looking to expand to the West Coast with a new entertainment division. That's where you come in. You both went to Harvard Law. You've both been very successful talent agents at William Morris..."

There was a knock on the door, followed by a young female cautiously poking her head into the room.

"There's a phone call for you, Mr. Reynolds."

"Who is it?" he asked, slightly irritated at his pitch being interrupted.

"It's your sister-in-law."

"Excuse me for a minute, will you?" he said to the men as he grabbed the phone in one corner of the room. "Cheryl. What's up?" And then, "I'm on my way."

The conversation lasted a total of three seconds. He turned back to the men at the table.

"Gentlemen, I'm really sorry, but I'm going to have to cut this short. My wife just went into labor back east with our first child, and I have to get on a plane."

"Congratulations," both men said in unison. They understood, but were also a little disappointed at the abrupt end of their meeting.

"Thank you. But before I go, let me leave you with one thought. Obviously, if the two of you come with us, you will help legitimize our firm on the entertainment front a lot quicker. But either way, we're going to expand our West Coast office. So my advice to you is to either climb aboard, or get off the tracks, because with or without you, the train is coming through."

The men weren't sure how to take the comment.

"Is that a threat, Mr. Reynolds?"

"No, gentlemen. *That...*is a fact. I'll be on a plane for the next five hours, but reachable after that. Have a great day."

An hour from the airport to the office for a five minute meeting, followed by another hour to get back to the airport, only to find that the departure board read *"Delayed"* next to its flight to New York City. Nick approached the counter.

"Can you tell me what the hold up is on the flight to New York? I just spoke to someone there and they said the weather is fine."

"It is fine there. It's Chicago where the weather is bad," the ticketing agent responded.

"Well, I'm not trying to get to Chicago."

"But Chicago is where your plane is coming from."

"Can you explain to me *why* my plane is coming from Chicago? Why wouldn't you use the same plane to go back and forth between New York and L.A.? That way, you wouldn't have three cities that are screwed up right now."

"We also wouldn't be able to have five direct flights a day between the two cities if we did it that way."

Even then, it boiled down to the almighty dollar. "Well, can you get me anywhere on the East Coast? My wife just went into labor."

She checked her computer.

"I could get you to Boston. But all flights from Boston to New York tonight are sold out.

"What about Newark?"

"New Jersey?" she asked incredulously, as if questioning why anyone would ever want to go there.

"Yes. I live in Connecticut. I'm just trying to find the quickest way home."

"We don't fly to New Jersey," she said with a scrunch of her nose.

"Then just get me to Boston," he answered impatiently.

A few hours later, his plane touched down at Logan Airport. He wondered how far along his wife was in labor or if she had already had the baby and he had missed it. She might never speak to him again if he didn't make it back on time.

Nick approached one of the agents from Hertz. He was puzzled that no one else was in line.

"Hello. I'd like to rent a car. One way with a drop off in Stamford, CT."

"I'm sorry, but we're sold out this weekend."

"Sold out? Wow. I guess I'll have to try Avis."

"I don't think you'll have much luck there either. All the agencies are sold out this weekend."

"Excuse me? Are you giving cars away?"

"Walter Payton and the Bears are in town to play the Patriots. Plus, there's the Harvard-Yale game, and Boston College's Homecoming."

"Good lord. Is there any other way to get to Connecticut tonight? Train perhaps?"

"Of course. Out of South Station."

"And how do I get to South Station?"

"A shuttle bus that picks up out front every half hour."

It was closer to an hour by the time he finally reached the train station. He called Cheryl from a nearby pay phone.

"I'm about to get on a train to Stamford. I'll take a cab to the hospital once I get there. I should be about three more hours. Tell her to hold on until then."

"I am most definitely *not* going to tell her that."

Nick stepped off the train in Connecticut and waved to a cab that promptly switched its sign to "OFF" and drove off. He appeared to flag down another one, but a lady stepped in front of him with a smile and jumped in. For the briefest of moments, he contemplated yanking the lady from the cab and throwing her to the ground, but common sense prevailed. The third time was the charm. He finally got one to stop.

The cab screeched to a halt in front of the hospital entrance. Nick threw some money at the driver and jumped out.

He raced to the front desk, barely pausing to get out the word, "Maternity???"

"Green wing. 5th Floor," the girl answered.

He ran to the elevators and when he saw that the closest one was on the 7th floor, he decided not to wait. Nick raced up the stairs instead and ran right by the door to his wife's room when he reached the 5th floor. He backpedaled once he realized it. His tie was almost completely undone. His button down was hanging out on all sides. He

was out of breath from having sprinted up five
flights of stairs.

Meanwhile, Jane was asleep in the bed. Cheryl
sat in a nearby chair holding a newborn baby boy
in her arms.

"Is everyone..." Nick panted, barely able to get
the words out, "Is everyone ok?"

"Everyone's fine," Cheryl smiled. "Mom and
the baby are both sleeping."

"She's going to kill me isn't she?"

"She'll get over it."

Cheryl stood. Walked towards him holding
the baby out for him to hold. "Let me introduce
you to your son. Jane said you both agreed on the
name Joshua."

"That's right. Joshua Nicholas."

She handed him over. "I'll let you two get
acquainted."

She left the room and Nick paced slowly back
and forth, scared to death like any new father
holding his son for the first time.

"You don't know it yet," he whispered in Josh's
ear, "But you're the luckiest baby here, because
you got the cute mom. Now, I know you're going
to take some crap from your friends when you get
older for having a cute mom, but it's ok. It'll be
worth it. Because none of them will have one as
smart, funny, and sweet as yours. She'll never let
anything bad happen to you on her watch. And
neither will I," he added. ~

Twelve years later, Nick and his son sat in silence as if they had both just drifted back from something too beautiful to describe.

"And did she get over it?" Josh asked.

"No, she never did. Not that I could blame her."

"Why though? You did everything you could to get back on time."

"I know. But the thing is, I never should have left. It wasn't the first time I had put work before family. And it wouldn't be the last. I always knew what the right thing to do was. I could just never get myself to do it."

"How come?"

"I guess I thought there'd be plenty of time to make it up to her and you later. But let this be the lesson you take from me. Life's funny. More often than not, it gives you a second chance. But every now and then, it gives you once in a lifetime opportunities. The birth of a child being one of them. And when one of those opportunities happen, you have to make them your priority or you'll spend the rest of your life trying to get back something you can't."

There was a light knock on the door. Jane poked her head inside. She seemed a little softer than before.

"How are we doing?" she asked.

"We're doing great," Nick answered.

"You almost ready to go?" she asked Josh.

"Not yet. We're listening to music," Josh answered with a differential nod toward his dad.

Nick winked at his son.

"Well, your dad's got to be pretty tired. Don't wear him out."

"I won't. I promise."

She left as the crooning of the Chairman of the Board began to play from the music box. Frank Sinatra's "*I Get a Kick Out of You.*"

"I love Frank. A voice that could melt butter," Nick mused as he closed his eyes once again.

VI
SUNDAY MORNINGS ˜ 1955

*B*ack in the 50's, long before the youth sports explosion that invaded every weekend, Sundays used to be family day, and the Reynolds were no different. Each Sunday began the same way with Nick's father setting the table for breakfast and making free squeezed orange juice by hand. Nick secretly hated the juice because it had too much pulp in it and little seeds he referred to as "tsi tsi's", which prevented him from gulping it down. But he never said anything because he didn't want to hurt his father's feelings. After all, it was the only thing his father ever successfully made in the kitchen. The choices for cereal were Cheerios, and well, Cheerios. If it was in season, he'd occasionally have some fresh peaches, raspberries or a sliced banana to go on top.

Shortly after breakfast, they made their way to church for the weekly battle of fortitude and will. They stood for what felt like several hours, but in reality was only about 45 minutes, side by side with 200 other people in a building built for 150. The only brush with fresh air came from the sliver-like openings of the stained glass windows, and even then, only if there was a large gust of wind outside.

The pews were made of wood, but felt like granite.

"You're not at the theatre. The pews aren't supposed to be comfortable," Nick's mother was fond of saying.

Mission accomplished in that case. The seats were so uncomfortable, they made standing seem like a better option.

Coffee in the church hall followed, where adults would complain to other adults about how awful their week had been. There were Stella Doro cookies for the children, and Nick was fairly certain that they tasted exactly like the bottom of his shoe would, if he decided to eat it. But the old ladies loved them, because they didn't crumble and turn to mush as soon as they dunked them in their coffee.

After withstanding a barrage of cheek pinches and kisses from women with more facial hair than his Uncle Harold, they eventually made it to his grandparents for some suspect food. The house always smelled like prune juice and tapioca pudding, the furniture was covered in plastic as if it was being preserved for the Smithsonian, and the floor model television had a base that was twice as big as the screen and three times as heavy.

"Why do we have to come here *every* week?" Nick wailed as he stood on the top step in front of the house.

"Because your grandmother isn't going to be with us forever."

"My friends are all playing football."

"I bet some of your friends wish their grandmothers were still alive."

"She makes me drink prune juice and eat tapioca pudding."

"There are an awful lot of people in this world that would kill to have prune juice and tapioca pudding."

"Can we give it to them then?"

"Very funny, smart guy."

"I mean, it would be selfish of us to keep it all for ourselves," Nick smirked.

"Now listen," his father began, "I'll give you a quarter if you dance with your grandmother today."

"No way. It's too embarrassing."

"She loves it when you dance. It makes her whole week." When he sensed he wasn't getting anywhere, he upped the offer. "Ok, fifty cents."

"It's *really* embarrassing."

"A buck."

"For two, you've got a deal."

"For two, you better dance like Fred Astaire."

Nick held out his hand.

"Do we have a deal?"

"Deal," his father agreed begrudgingly as he shook it. "We'll put the two bucks toward your law school degree."

Nick's dad turned on the AM radio in the living room and motioned for Nick to get moving. Frank Sinatra's "*I Get a Kick Out of You*" was the first song that played.

Nick walked over to his grandmother and held out his hand for her to dance with him. She smiled and happily joined him on the makeshift dance floor in the living room. They rocked back and forth and soon began swinging and spinning around the room.

About halfway through the song, Nick reached out with an arm and *pulled* his father toward his mother. They were soon all dancing. His father was actually pretty smooth in his own right--dancing and laughing as the song came to an end. Even Nick was smiling. He seemed to have forgotten for a moment that he was being paid.

But only for a moment, before he held his hand out behind his back. His father slipped two dollars into it.

~

Back in the present, Nick smiled a sad smile as the last lyrical stylings of Frank Sinatra faded away from the music box.

"How'd you get to be such a good dancer?" Josh asked.

"My parents made me take dancing classes from 2nd grade through 8th grade."

"That must have been awful."

"It was," Nick chuckled faintly. "But it helped me make a few bucks."

"Do you miss your grandmother?" Josh asked curiously.

Nick paused for a moment before answering.

"A day rarely passes where I don't think about her. But up until today, I've had a hard time making out her face."

"How come?"

"Because it's been a while since I've seen it.

You know, it's funny. My parents used to have to drag me kicking and screaming to visit my grandparents. And yet, I'd give just about anything I have right now to be able to hear my grandmother's laugh one more time. Her whole body would shake when she laughed. It was so contagious."

"I wish I could have known her."

"Me too, pal. Me too. Make sure you appreciate people while they are still around, because by the time you realize how important they are to you, it's usually too late. In fact, that's another life lesson for you. I'm giving you gems here. You should probably be writing them down."

"I'll remember them. Is that why you wanted to see me? Before it was too late?"

"I've always wanted to see you, pal. I just kind of screwed things up."

"How come?"

Once again those two simple words led to a complicated answer.

"Because that's what I do. That and help people who don't deserve it."

Josh was puzzled. "Like who?"

"Like my idiot clients."

VII
MISGUIDED LOYALTY~

Nick Reynolds didn't graduate at the top of his law school class at Syracuse, but he could have if he didn't need to work three jobs to pay for it. During meal times, he slopped dishes at one of the dining halls, which was a gruesome job that entailed scraping some of the most horrific piles of uneaten food off plates before putting them in the dishwasher. Cereal with mashed potatoes. Granola on top of spaghetti. Ketchup, mustard, mayonnaise and salad dressing all mixed together. In the late afternoons, he worked for a small law firm in the city doing research for criminal cases they were trying. It was there that he learned more about the law than in any class he took.

Late night he worked as a bartender at a dive college bar. He wasn't flinging bottles of vodka over his shoulder. Just beer, wine, and the occasional screwdriver or Bloody Mary. The individual tips were usually not great, but there were plenty of them as the bar was packed Thursday through Monday nights. Tuesdays and Wednesdays were the days he caught up on his class work. He was thankful for his photographic memory that helped him survive.

It was all a far cry from his undergraduate days where his parents paid for school and he didn't need to work. He only needed to attend the occasional class, play basketball for the Fighting Irish, and court the girls from St. Mary's College, the all girls school across the road, since Notre Dame didn't admit women until his senior year.

He landed a job at the Public Defender's Office in his hometown of Stamford, three months after graduating from law school. His father knew a guy who knew a guy, who knew a guy, who knew the cousin of a guy, who once worked for the State's Assistant District Attorney. That's how people got jobs back then. Not by job fairs or sending out 2,000 letters.

~

Nick sat behind a modest desk inside an even more modest office. A small transistor radio quietly played The Byrds "*Mr. Tambourine Man*" in the background. After a brief knock on the door, it was thrown open and a man entered. He tossed a folder on Nick's desk. Charlie O'Brien was Nick's boss.

"Got a case for you," Charlie said. "Just came in."

"What is it?" Nick asked as he flipped open the folder.

"Grand theft auto. Guy allegedly stole a car from outside the Palace Theatre and drove it to a strip club outside of town where he parked it in a no parking zone and got it towed."

"Did he do it?"

"Course he did it. We've never had a client who didn't."

"What do you want me to do with the case? Plead it out?"

"I want you to win," Charlie smiled as he tapped Nick's desk twice before leaving.

First stop was the Palace Theatre parking lot to speak to the attendant. He was about Nick's age, give or take a year or two either way.

"How ya doin? My name is Nick Reynolds. I'm representing a guy named Robert Lyons. He's accused of stealing a car from this lot Tuesday night. I was wondering if I could ask you a few questions."

"Sure," the attendant answered. "The Prosecutors were already here."

"When did you know the car was missing?"

"When the owners came out of the theatre and couldn't find it."

"So you didn't see anybody actually take it?"

"No. But there are a lot of cars here and they're not all visible from the booth."

"Is there more than one exit here?" Nick asked as he looked around the lot.

"No. Just this one."

"Then wouldn't someone have to show you a ticket before they can leave?

"They pay on the way in."

"Then how do they get out?"

"With a ticket they're given on the way in. Most people leave the ticket in the car even though we tell them not to."

"But they still have to drive right by you..."

"Yes, but I could have been taking money from another customer who was on their way in."

"Any idea then what made the police think Mr. Lyons stole the car?"

"Don't know. Guess they must have seen him driving it."

"Have *you* ever seen Mr. Lyons before?"

"Plenty of times," the attendant nodded. "He hangs around this area all the time. He sometimes plays craps with the other parking lot guys."

"Was he playing that night?"

"Yeah."

"Did the prosecution ask you that?"

"Nope."

"Well, I'm not asking you to lie, but if that doesn't come up in court, I'd appreciate it if you didn't volunteer that information."

The attendant clearly didn't like his shitty job much what with the smell of gas fumes and rude people, but he also couldn't afford to lose it.

"No problem," he said at last after thinking it over. "If they don't ask, I won't tell. I like Rob well enough."

There was nothing more seedy than a seedy strip club in the daytime. Beer stains, dirt and dust were far more visible without the fluorescent lighting and strobe. The manager was a leathery looking guy in his 40's. He smoked a cigarette while he "cleaned" a few glasses behind the bar.

"I'm Nick Reynolds," Nick said, careful not to touch anything. "I'm with the Public Defender's office and wanted to ask you a few questions about Robert Lyons."

"Who?"

"A customer of yours who was arrested here a couple of nights ago."

"Ohhh. The car thief."

"Alleged car thief," Nick smiled.

"Yeah. Whatever that means. If it means he stole a car, then I know who you're talking about."

"You seem pretty sure of that."

"Guy's a dirtbag. He's always grabbing the girls. I've had to throw him out of here three or four times."

"Then why do you keep letting him in?"

"I only let him in on slow nights."

"And Tuesday was a slow night?"

"It was a Tuesday," the manager said with an expression that said "*duhh*".

"Well, if it was a slow night, then I suppose someone saw him drive up in the stolen car?"

"Not exactly."

"So what makes you so sure he's guilty then?"

"Well, they did take him away in handcuffs."

The man would definitely be what was categorized as a hostile witness if this case came to trial.

"But no one saw him drive up in the car."

"True. But when I noticed the car in the no parking zone, I announced that it needed to be moved or it would get towed."

"And did he go outside?"

"No. I think he was in the back with one of the girls. But when he came out, someone must have told him because he rushed to the door."

"And did he say it was his car?"

"Nope. He just shrugged and sat back down."

"So it could have been anyone in here then that drove up in that car."

"Cops found the keys to the car in his jacket pocket," the manager smiled.

After a morning chasing his tail, it was time to go see his client. Robert Lyons had long, scraggily hair, an uneven mustache and beard, and beady eyes. Nick sat across from him in the meeting room. Lyons eyed him suspiciously, although it should probably have been the other way around.

"The public defender's office assigned me to your case," Nick began. "Now, I'm not even going to ask you if you did it, because quite frankly, I don't want to know. What I can tell you is that no one saw you driving the car out of the lot, and no one saw you driving it up to the strip club. What they do have on you is that several people saw you looking for the car after it was towed..."

"I wasn't looking for it. I was having a cigarette," Lyons responded.

"Then how'd you get there that night?"

"Took a cab."

"The cab company will have a record of a fare going there, if there was in fact one."

"There was one."

"And were you in it?"

"I told you I was."

"Think the driver would remember you?"

"I wouldn't remember *him.*"

Nick nodded. It was not far fetched to believe that a man who liked to play craps with parking lot attendants and hang out at strip clubs was rolling the dice on "someone" having taken a cab to the club that night. Fair enough. He would deal with that later.

"Oh. One more thing. There is the issue of the cops finding the car keys in your jacket pocket."

"Somebody must have put them there. My jacket was hanging on a chair while I was in the back."

"Of course they must have. We'll go with that."

Lyons sensed that Nick still didn't believe him.

"If I knew they were there, don't you think I would have tossed the keys on the floor somewhere in the bar so they couldn't pin it on me?"

The response would have been more plausible coming from someone Nick thought was bright enough to think that way.

"Well, here's the thing, Robert. They've got a host of circumstantial evidence against you. This case is going to ride on how believable you appear to be. And frankly, you look like a degenerate who would steal a car and go to a strip club. You own a suit?"

"Do I look like I own a suit?"

"I'll take that as a "nooo". I'll bring you one of mine. And I'm going to get my barber in here to give you a cut and a shave. Your mother live in the area?"

"My mother hates me."

"That...is not surprising at all. Well, we've got to find someone to make you look a bit more sympathetic. I'll work on that."

After ten people turned him down to "imply" they were Robert Lyons' mother in court, Nick finally got a yes from an older lady that lived in his apartment complex.

Only a handful of people were inside the courtroom on the day of the trial, in addition to the lawyers. A clean-cut Robert Lyons walked in wearing a smart navy suit, pressed white shirt and a patriotic red, white and blue tie. He looked like a banker. Sitting behind him was Nick's kindly looking neighbor. White hair, knit button-down sweater. She looked like Mary Werth from the Lil Abner comic strip.

"Who's the corpse?" Lyons asked Nick.

"A sweet old lady who lives in the apartment above me."

"What's she doing here?"

"Trying to save your ass and get me a promotion at the same time. So turn around and smile at her."

When Lyons did, you could almost *feel* the sympathy pouring out of the jury box.

~

Josh looked at his father wide-eyed. "Was he guilty?"

"The jury found him not guilty," Nick answered. "And there's a life lesson in it for you."

"Don't judge a book by its cover?"

"Hell no. The guy was guilty as hell. Six

months later Robert Lyons was arrested for shooting a convenience store clerk during a robbery. And while he was on trial, he become the only person to ever escape from the Fairfield County Jail by climbing out through the skylight. They found him two weeks later living in the basement of some older couple's house in South Carolina."

"Did you represent him the second time?"

"Yup. And the third time. And the 4th."

"So if he kept getting arrested, where's the life lesson in that?"

"Give people the benefit of the doubt. Usually they'll end up disappointing you, but every once in a while, they'll surprise you, and that's what makes life worth living."

Mr. Tambourine Man ended and Nick was suddenly distracted by the next song out of the music box.

"I haven't heard this song in forever," he reminisced. "I was in high school when it came out."

And the room suddenly became a blur once again.

VIII
YOU WIN, YOU LOSE~1965

*I*t was Homecoming in 1965. The boys wore jackets, ties, white shirts and loafers. The girls wore knee-high dresses, bobby socks and Buster Brown shoes. The Shirelles, *"Will You Love Me Tomorrow?"* was playing over the speakers as about three dozen couples danced. More than five dozen other girls were waiting while an equal number of boys decided who they wanted to ask.

Sixteen-year-old Nick Reynolds stood with three friends by the punch bowl. Peter Cook was tall, sharp-witted and ruggedly handsome. Mike Shaw was tall and rugged as well. He could have been Peter's bookend. Jim Roberts was shorter and quieter than the other two.

"All right. Fifteen bucks for the person who gets the furthest with a girl tonight. Five bucks each from the three losers," Peter said.

"How will we know?" Mike asked.

"If you don't know how far you got, then you've got more problems than I thought."

"I *meant*, dumbass, how are we going to know how far someone *else* has gotten? What proof are we going to have?"

"You'll have to give a very vivid description of the events. We'll know if you're lying. Well, Jim might not, but the rest of us will. Besides, it's a gentlemen's bet. So who's in?" Peter explained.

"Sounds like a real gentlemen's bet," Mike chuckled, "but I'm in."

"Me too," Nick said.

"Jim?" Peter asked.

"No thanks. I'm waiting."

"Waiting? For what?"

"For the right girl."

"Jimbo, you'll never get a hit if you wait for the ball to hit the bat. But whatever. Ok, the bet is ten bucks then. Now, if you'll excuse me, Jenny Doyle has been eyeing me all night."

Jenny was a petite, blonde, cheerleader type, with the sort of smile that should have been in a television commercial.

"I'm going after Amanda Perkins," Mike said.

They both walked off to ask the respective girls to dance. Both girls accepted.

"How can you compete with those guys?" Jim asked.

"Because they may be good-looking and outgoing, but they're not very bright. Pretty girls aren't going to put out because they don't have to. And ugly girls aren't going to put out either, because they're always suspicious of your motives. The ones to go after are the chubby ones, because they're just pretty enough to believe you like them, but heavy enough that they'll be grateful," Nick reasoned.

Nick winked as he headed off towards Edna

Kowalski. She wasn't what someone would describe as homely, but she wasn't exactly a pin up either. She was what was commonly described as "big-boned".

She accepted his offer to dance. Formally at first, but she began to close the gap between them a couple of inches at a time. Pretty soon, she had her head resting on his shoulder. Two songs later, Nick was leading her down an otherwise empty school hallway.

"I'm so glad you asked me to dance," Edna said. "I've wanted to date you ever since we were freshmen. I guess that was only two years ago, but it seems like a whole lot longer. It's funny. You were in a dream I had the other night. This is fate."

If Nick was actually listening to her, he might have felt guilty for making her part of a bet, but he kept focused on the task at hand. He kept checking the classroom doors until he found one that was unlocked.

"And I think it's so sweet that you want our first kiss to be in the room where we first had class together," she continued.

He held open the door for her, while Jimmy watched in awe from the other end of the hallway.

"My hero," Jimmy said to himself.

Once inside, Nick fought the battle within himself and finally mustered up the courage to make his move. After all, ten bucks wasn't chump change.

He decided on the "arm stretch" move. He

reached out as if he was stretching, only to have his arm land on her shoulders. She did the rest. Pulled him in tight, while he fumbled around the back of her dress for the zipper. Nick tugged and tugged on it until the dress *ripped* and fell to her ankles. She didn't even seem to mind—until she heard some rustling behind a bookcase.

Peter, Mike, Jenny and Amanda poked their heads around the corner. They were all completely dressed. Edna screamed and ran from the room, trying to pull her dress back up as she went. The two girls ran after her. Peter and Mike were laughing uncontrollably. Peter held out his hand.

"Give me your five bucks."

Mike did so without hesitation. Peter added his five and handed it over to Nick.

"But I didn't even touch her breasts," Nick said.

"Listen. Any guy who'd even consider fooling around with Edna Kowalski deserves the money," Peter deadpanned as Mike and he started laughing again.

"Best five bucks I've ever spent," Mike laughed.

Nick held the ten dollars in the open palm of his hand, looking like he *lost* the bet.

~

Present day Nick shook his head. Josh was smiling.

"So I take it the life lesson is that pretty girls aren't going to put out—whatever that means— because they don't have to. And ugly girls aren't going to put out either, because they're always suspicious. The ones to go after are the chubby ones."

"No, pal," his father corrected. "The life lesson is don't kiss fat girls, but if you do, make sure there are no witnesses."

IX
A LIFE FOREVER CHANGED ˜

Nick's brother, Dan, had a female friend, Cheryl Harrison, who had a younger sister, Jane, who Nick had seen once from a distance and couldn't take his eyes off. But before he got the chance to actually speak to her, his ride decided to leave the party. He wasn't too worried, because he figured Cheryl could set him up with her sister another time.

Another time ended up being two quasi-boyfriends and three months before she finally agreed. She wasn't without her reservations. Nick was older for starters. He was a 28 year old lawyer with a reputation as a smooth talker, while Jane was a no nonsense recent college graduate who wasn't easily smooth talked and had aspirations of her own.

The first date needed to be on neutral ground so they agreed on New York City, which was a thirty minute train ride away. Nick always preferred dinner and a movie for a first date in case his date was boring so that the silence of the movie theatre could act as a welcome relief. They settled on dinner at a family owned diner in midtown. It was clean, the service was good, the food even better, and they had the best milkshakes for three states. At least that's what they advertised. Nick and Jane were quickly seated at a side booth mid restaurant, which was a great spot for people watching, which both, unbeknownst to each other, were prone to doing. Van Morrison's "*Sweet Thing*" was playing out of the jukebox.

"Best shakes for three states," Nick mused as he read a sign on the front window. "I wonder which direction they're talking about. Connecticut, Rhode Island and Massachusetts? Connecticut, Massachusetts and New Hampshire? Pennsylvania, Ohio and Kentucky? Or New Jersey, Delaware and Maryland?"

"I'm not really sure," Jane answered in a measured tone that indicated she was reconsidering her decision to go out with him.

"And if it was all of the above, wouldn't that mean they had the best shakes for 10 states? And if it isn't all of the above, then basically they're lying," he continued.

"Uh huh..." was all she could muster for a response.

"I think about things like that. Must be the lawyer in me."

"Must be."

"So tell me what it was that finally convinced you to go out with me after all this time? I mean obviously I'm really good looking, but you probably saw that for yourself three months ago."

"Honestly? Cheryl told me you had a good sense of humor," she answered. She didn't tell her that he was also certifiably nuts. She left that part out. In the early date grade, Nick had received a D-. The D was for being boring and conceited. The minus for not shutting up.

"I think that's actually understating it a bit," Nick countered. "I have an *excellent* sense of humor." Nick gave himself an early date grade of an A+. The A for being observant and funny. The plus for unique. "Oh my god!" Nick said in a voice that was louder than expected for a public place. "Winston Churchill's here!"

Jane looked over at a man with a distant resemblance to him. Large, bald head. Glasses. But he's dressed in a polyester suit.

"Umm, Winston Churchill is dead. He died twelve years ago."

"Ahhh. Cheryl hasn't told you about The Game."

"The Game?" Jane's interest was piqued for the first time.

"The People Game. When you're out in public you look for people that resemble another person. It doesn't have to be someone famous. It could be your uncle or a friend. And they shouldn't be dead ringers either. They should only share one quality with the other person. And the rest of their characteristics should actually be the opposite. For example, if a white man in a track suit walked in, that was old and unathletic looking, you'd say, "Hey, it's Bob Hayes! Or if you saw an older woman with poofy, wavy sandy brown hair, you'd say, 'Queen Elizabeth!' It's like creating a real life caricature."

"I want to try."

"Be my guest. But make sure you're enthusiastic. It's all in the sale."

She looked around the room.

"Look! Gordon Liddy!" she screamed.

"Yeah...that doesn't quite work."

"Why not??" she asked, offended.

"Because it *is* Gordon Liddy."

"Really?"

"Pretty sure."

"Jerry Lewis!" she tried, pointing to an Asian man with glasses, who actually looked a bit like the character Lewis played in "*Hollywood or Bust*".

"That's not bad," Nick chuckled. "But not as good as if you had said, "Hey, it's Jerry LEE Lewis!"

He motioned with his head toward a man in his 70's with a teenage girl.

"That's a man and his granddaughter," she laughed in spite of her efforts not to. "You're bad. So tell me something."

"Fire away. What do you want to know?"

"Why law?"

"Because I like to argue."

"That I can see. But what I meant was why not take over your dad's ice cream parlor? Seems like it would have been the easy thing to do."

"And that's the reason why I didn't."

"Boys and their fathers. They never seem to want to follow in their footsteps. I guess they don't think it's good enough for them."

"Actually, I think the opposite is true. Most of the time they don't feel like they could live up to them, so they try to find some other way to make their mark in the world."

"Is that what you're doing?"

"Sort of. I mean I could never be my father. He's a great man. Fortunately, I did get most of his best qualities. His good looks. His charm. His brains. His sense of humor."

"His modesty?"

"No, I think that must have skipped a generation. Dan pretty much thinks he's great too."

"Oh lord."

"What about you? What are your life plans? I hear all the time how brilliant you are."

"Just to find a nice guy and raise a family I suppose."

"That's it?"

"I think that's quite a bit actually."

"I didn't mean it like that. Of course it is. I just thought maybe you wanted more."

"What more is there?" she asked steadfastly.

"Fair enough. Oh my god! Cheryl never told me you had a twin!"

Jane spun around in time to see a woman wearing the same sweater she is—except it's about three sizes larger.

"That's not funny."

"Then why are you laughing?"

"I don't know!" she continued to laugh.

"Let me help you. It's because I'm funny, that's why."

"I don't know about funny. Old maybe," she smirked.

"Old?" he said defensively.

"Just how old are you anyway?"

"28."

"28?! You'd be in a wheelchair by the time our kids hit nursery school."

"We just formally met tonight and we're already having kids?! Slow it down there, sweet thing."

The waitress dropped off the bill at that moment.

"No rush at all, but I'll take it when you're ready," she said.

He handed it right back to her without even looking at it.

"I'm ready," Nick smiled.

She didn't know quite how to take it.

"I'm kidding. My daughter will take care of it."

Nick and Jane walked arm in arm down the street.

"Thanks for dinner," she said, clearly more comfortable now.

"You're very welcome. It wasn't exactly Tavern on the Green," Nick answered followed by a slightly awkward pause. "You know, I've got a bone to pick with Cheryl."

"Why's that?"

"Because she should have warned me how blue your eyes were. I have to be honest. I've been so distracted by them, I haven't listened to a single thing you've said all night."

Jane stopped walking. "I don't know whether to be insulted or flattered."

"Flattered."

She blushed. Then leaned in and kissed him on the cheek. "Thank you," she said before suddenly adding,

"Nick!"

He looked puzzled.

"Nick!" she yelled again.

"Why are you shouting?" he asked. "I'm right in front of you."

"Nick!" she yelled for a third time.

This time he turned to see what she was looking at.

A man in his late 70's, walking with a cane, wearing a similar shirt to the one Nick had on.

Nick nodded and smiled wryly. "I never should have introduced you to The Game."

~

Josh laughed at the thought of his mother pulling one over on his father. "Hard to picture mom joking," Josh said.

"Oh, she had a great sense of humor. We used to laugh and laugh. Sometimes we were the only two people in the room laughing, but we had a lot of fun."

"She's always so serious now."

"Probably because she has to be. But I'm convinced that my sense of humor is what won her over. My father always used to say that a sense of humor is the most valuable thing you can ever get for free. People like them. Women *love* them."

The song on the music box changed again.

"This was your mom and my wedding song."

"I know. James Taylor. She still listens to it

sometimes."

"She does?"

"Yeah. Usually when she's in a bad mood."

"Interesting."

"How long did you guys date before getting married?" Josh asked.

"We were engaged three months from our first date. And married two months after that."

"That's pretty quick isn't it?"

"Maybe for some people. But I would have done it after five *minutes*."

"I wish I could have been at your wedding."

"Well, that would have been a little like putting the cart before the horse, but you almost were, pal. You were born nine months later. We think you were conceived on our wedding night."

~

About 150 of their closest friends and family attended Nick and Jane's wedding. They would later describe it as a real life picture show of their lives with so many people from different parts of their lives. High school. College. Law school. Next door neighbors. Relatives they hadn't seen in years.

It took place at a vineyard in Northeastern Connecticut. They knew that is where they wanted to have it the moment they saw it. Fortunately, the weather was uncharacteristically comfortable for mid-August, which was a saving grace in the small church that didn't have much ventilation.

It was considered a bit unusual for the bride or groom to speak at a wedding, but Nick was never one to shy away from an open microphone. He grabbed the mic like he was about to give a comedy routine, which in some respects, he was.

"First of all, I want to thank everyone for coming today. It's great seeing old friends and family--and by that I should add that I'm not saying you *are* old, just that we've known you a long time-- anyway, it's great seeing old friends together with new ones. Over the last couple of months since Jane and I got engaged, I've been asked one question far more than any other. And that is, you're both so young. Why get married now? My response has always been one word. Fairness. You see, four of my friends have gotten married in the last year, and I just didn't think it was fair for one person to continue to enjoy life unfettered by responsibility, so I thought it was only fair that I join their suffering."

The crowd roared while Jane rolled her eyes. She had expected him to say something like that.

"At any rate, I've actually known Jane's sister Cheryl through my brother Dan, for about ten years, and I'd been begging her to set me up with her little sister for several months before she finally relented. If Jane only knew that she was sold out for a couple of upper deck Springsteen tickets, she might not be speaking to her sister right now. Did I just say that out loud?"

More laughter.

"So our first date was to the Midtown Diner on 52nd Street in New York City. No one can say I'm not a big spender, but after the Springsteen tickets, it was about all I could afford." He paused for laughter. "At least we were joined for dinner by Winston Churchill, Jerry Lewis and Jerry Lee Lewis."

Nick and Jane shared a smile.

"You know, I once asked my buddy, Jimmy, who's here tonight with his lovely wife Amy, how he knew she was the right one. His answer was simple. "You just know," he said. And I remember thinking at the time, *Gee, thanks pal, that doesn't really help me at all.* But from the moment I watched Jane fold herself Indian-style into a chair that was clearly not meant to sit Indian-style in, and looked into her blue eyes for the first time, Jimmy Roberts became Socrates to me."

There was a collective "Awwwww" from the audience.

"So I returned home that night," Nick continued, "even though Jane practically begged me to sneak into her parents' house and stay with her..."

She shook her head to let their guests know that she "most certainly did not".

"....and I called Jimmy to tell him I had found the girl I was going to marry."

More "Awwws".

"So, tonight, I'd like to congratulate myself—"

The crowd roared with laughter.

"--for not only being a prophet, but for somehow finding a way to convince this smart, funny, sweet and
beautiful girl to spend the rest of her life with me."

Most of the women had tears in their eyes. The men, not so much.

"And we can't thank all of you enough for sharing the start of it with us, but we'd certainly like to try. Thank you so very, very much."

He handed the microphone to the leader of the band and shook several dozen hands on his way back to his seat, where he and Jane shared a kiss.

"We'd like to ask Nick and Jane to now come onto the dance floor for their first dance as a married couple," the bandleader said.

James Taylor's *"Something in the Way She Moves"* began to play as they slow danced their way around the dance floor.

~

Nick and Josh both looked as if they were in a different world. Their heads swaying back and forth to the music as if they were following people's motions. Not until the song ended, did they open their eyes.

"Mom looked really pretty," Josh said at last, breaking the silence.

"You mean today? Yes, she does."

"No, at the wedding."

"What do you mean?"

"I could see her."

"What do you mean you could see her?" Nick asked, confused now.

"I could see all of you. As soon as the music started, I could see everything. I've been able to see everything all day. Mom's dress was white and long."

Nick shrugged unconvinced. So was every bride's dress.

"You had on a white tuxedo with black pants."

"Long tie or bow tie?"

"Bow tie."

"Cummerbund or vest?"

"Vest."

"You've probably seen pictures," Nick reasoned.

"The waitress who served you on your first date with mom had long, big circley earrings. And she had a tattoo on her shoulder that said "Peace before War.""

Nick sat up a little straighter. There was no way Josh could have known that. He hadn't remembered it himself until just then.

"What color was the dress my grandmother was wearing when I danced with her?"

"Brown checkered."

Nick continued his investigation. "And her shoes?"

"Brown. With laces and thick soles."

"Holy crap, Joshey. I thought I was starting to hallucinate. Everything seemed so vivid. People I hadn't seen in years whose faces I have long forgotten, were suddenly so clear. Where did you get this music box??"

"Big Al's."

"The pawn shop?"

Josh nodded.

"Well, I've never really considered Big Al's to be a magical place, but make no mistake about it, there is definitely some magic in this box!"

Jane stuck her head into the bedroom at that moment. "Josh, I think we should let your dad get some rest."

"Do I have to? We're having fun."

"Yes, he needs his rest. But you can come back again."

Before you go, I've got a little something for you," Nick said.

He reached into the nightstand next to his bed and removed a neatly wrapped package.

"Happy Birthday, pal," Nick said as he handed it to his son.

"Should I open it now?"

"Why don't you open it at home?"

"Ok. Bye, dad. I'll come by again soon."

"How about tomorrow?" Nick asked.

"Mom?" Josh turned to his mother hopefully.

"Tomorrow after school," she answered.

"And thank you for the music box," Nick said. "It's the best present I've ever been given."

Josh could barely wait to open the present from his father until he got home. He practically leaped from the car and raced to the door, urging his mother to hurry up. Once he was safely alone in the confines of his own room, he took the wrapping paper off and folded it neatly next to him on the bed. Josh removed a portable CD player from the box along with a CD for The Beatles album "Rubber Soul". There was also a specially made card. On the outside was a picture of Nick and Josh playing basketball in the driveway when Josh was six.

Inside the card was a handwritten message.

"Dear Josh, I was looking through some old

pictures recently and thought you might like a copy of this one. I love it myself. As for the present, it's a state of the art portable CD player. You can take it with you anywhere. The CD is a classic. The Beatles sound so clear digitally. Listen to the song "In My Life". I know I haven't been the best dad, but I wanted you to know on your birthday, that you've always been the best son a father could ask for. Happy Birthday, pal. I love you. Dad."

Josh wiped a tear from his eye as he played the song. There was something complicated about the relationship between a father and son. It was a bond built over time, but fortified by the quality of time spent.

X
GUIDED LOYALTY~

*J*osh could barely make it through the next day at school, because he was so excited to see his father after it, and ask all the questions he had long wanted to ask. He wanted to learn who his father was. What was he like? What did people think of him? Why did he do some of the things he did? Would he make different choices if he had the chance to? So many questions. And he knew his time for answers was getting slimmer by the minute, which is why he literally sprinted for his mom's car as soon as the final bell signaled the end of the school day. There would be no snack on this day, no changing of clothes. Just straight to his father's house.

Nick was actually seated in a chair in his bedroom when he arrived, and appeared to have more color in his face. As if he had been invigorated somehow by re-connecting with his son.

"Thanks for coming, pal. And thanks for bringing him, Jane," Nick said.

"He wanted to come. It's all he's talked about since yesterday. I'll just do some work in the living room. Let me know if you need anything."

"Thank you."

"Well...?" Josh asked excitedly.

"Well, what?" was Nick's cheeky response.

"Are we going to listen to some music?"

"Sure, if you'd like to."

"Where is it?! Where's the music box?"

"You mean this thing?" Nick asked with a
smile, pulling it out from behind the chair.

"Yes!"

"I've waited all day for this," Nick said. "It
only seems to work if we are both here."

"Well, I'm here now."

"Then do the honors. Press play."

"*The Fool on the Hill*" begins to play. It
captures Nick's attention the way every Beatles
song did. "Can't have a mix tape without the
Beatles. This song always reminds me of your
Uncle Rob," he said with a shake of his head. "He
was a piece of work. Still is. One night in college,
I was sitting on a bench by the lake on campus with
my girlfriend when TP comes running up. He's
jogging and he waves and then picks up the pace to
impress us. The problem is he blows right past us
and hurdles the bushes that surround the lake and
lands directly into the water! Turns out old TP
didn't have his contacts in and thought the lake was
a wet parking lot."

"Why do you always call him TP if his name is
Rob?" Josh laughed.

"Our first day of college our freshmen year, TP
decided to go to the bathroom in the dorm. And
he put toilet paper all over the seat before he sat

down."

"Why did he do that?"

"Well, he was used to nice clean bathrooms at home I guess. His mom was kind of like yours. But in college, you share a bathroom with like 20 other guys, so it can get kind of gross. Anyway, it wouldn't have been a big deal if he had just flushed the paper down the toilet when he was done. But instead, he decided to just let it fall to the floor. Sure enough, one of the upper classmen came in after him and from that moment on, he was TP."

"I suppose the life lesson is to always put toilet paper on the seat in a public bathroom, but make sure to flush it when I'm done?" Josh asked.

"That's not so much a life lesson, pal, as sound advice," Nick laughed. "But I tell you what. As much as Uncle Rob has always been a goofy bastard, he's always been brilliant."

~

Nick was seated at a conference table with another man. Rob Kindle was also 30, with straight dark hair, glasses, pale skin. He was a bit awkward looking, but one of those guys that if they went through a makeover, people would be amazed at how good looking he had the potential to be. It just didn't come without effort.

"They might be in violation of the non-compete clause—UNLESS—he dissolves his company first and lets his employees go to work for the other company, and he goes to work for them in a completely unrelated department," Rob said.

"I like it," Nick nodded.

The intercom buzzed.

"Nick. Brad wants to see you," his secretary said.

"Tell him I'm on my way." And then to Rob, "Partner day. The day we've both been waiting for."

"I don't know, Nick. I'm sure you'll make it. But they don't like me much."

"No one likes you when they first meet you, but you grow on people after a while."

"Gee, thanks."

"Don't worry. You'll make it."

"And if I don't?"

"You'll make it," Nick repeated.

Brad Carter was the Senior Partner of the firm, Carter, Mellman & Jones. He was in his mid-50's, slickly distinguished looking, with a suit that was worth more than Nick's car.

"Nick! Big day. Big news," Brad greeted him with the enthusiasm of long-lost friends.

"For?"

"For you of course!" he said before adding with emphasis, "*Partner.*"

"Really?"

"C'mon. You can't be that surprised. Granted, you're the youngest partner we've ever had, but you deserve it. You've brought in a *lot* of business."

"That's only because I have a lot of relatives who are criminals. Can I ask who else made it?"

"The usual suspects. Sean. Kevin. Tom."

"Rob?"

"Rob isn't exactly partner material."

"He's a very good lawyer. I wouldn't have won several of my cases without him. You wouldn't have won the Ford brake recall case without him."

"He's just not the face we want to put forth as a partner."

"What does that even mean?"

"He has no people skills, Nick. You know that."

"That's just until you get to know him."

"We don't have time for people to get to know him. He's fine if we give him a case, but he doesn't bring in any business on his own. Plus Ron and Jim don't like him."

"If he doesn't make partner, that means you're going to let him go," Nick said.

When Brad didn't answer him, he knew he was correct.

Nick hesitated for just a moment before continuing, "Yeah, I don't think that's going to work."

"What's not going to work?"

"Me, at this firm, without TP."

"The guy's nickname is TP for god's sake. Don't hitch your wagon to an anchor. Do the right thing here."

"I'm about to."

"Nick. C'mon. You're on the fast track. Don't throw that away."

"Brad, there's this thing called loyalty. Some people believe in it. Others don't. I don't begrudge those who don't, but I'm also not about to sell out, because I *do* believe in it. Sorry, Brad.

It's either both of us, or neither of us."

"Ronnie said that would be your response. I told him there was no way you were that stupid. Guess I was wrong."

"Don't confuse loyalty with stupidity. Sometimes it's difficult to see the forest through the trees," Nick answered. "But don't be so hard on yourself. You'll get there someday."

Nick took the longest way possible home as he tried to play out how this same conversation would go with his wife. There were two likely responses and neither would be pleasant. He secretly hoped she had forgotten that today was the day, but when he walked through the door to find Jane anxiously waiting, he knew that wasn't the case.

"Well?" she asked.

"Well what?"

"You know very well, well what. What happened? Did you make partner?"

"Let's just say that's not going to work out exactly the way we had hoped."

"What do you mean? They passed you over?!! You bring in more business than Brad Carter! The hell with them! Take your clients to another firm!" she exclaimed.

"Glad you feel that way."

"I just can't believe they passed you over."

"Well, they didn't exactly pass me over. They passed TP over. So I turned them down."

"You did WHAT???"

"I turned them down. Told them it was both of us or neither of us. They thought neither sounded better."

"Why on earth would you do that?! TP is not your responsibility."

"Actually he is. Because I'm the one who brought him to that firm. And he deserved to make partner."

"I'm sure he did, and I'm sorry for that, but he isn't your responsibility. Your family is. What are you going to say to your son when he wonders why you put your friend before your family?"

"That friend also *is* family. And when he asks, I'm going to tell him that I couldn't just cut his godfather loose. I think he'll understand."

"Not when we can't afford to send him to the college he wants to go to."

"We'll be able to. TP and I are going to start our own firm. I took the client roster before I left and I've already called my biggest clients. They're all coming with me."

"Do you think that's a smart thing to do?"

"Two minutes ago you told me I should take my clients and tell Brad to shove it."

"I said you should take them to another firm. And that was when I thought they had turned YOU down. Not the other way around."

"Everything will be fine."

"You've said yourself that TP doesn't bring in any clients of his own. So basically, you'll be splitting up your clients with him."

"With an eighth of the overhead."

"I don't understand you. TP wouldn't give you half a sandwich, much less half his client roster."

"Relax. I don't do anything to lose. Reynolds

men win. It's what we do."

Jane cracked half a smile. "Is that so?"

"I got you to marry me didn't I?" Nick winked.

~

"I'm glad you stood up for Uncle Rob," Josh said once the song had ended.

"Joshey. Over the course of your life, you'll only meet a handful of people that you really connect with and trust. When you find them, hang on to them, and above all else, be loyal. Any asshole can look out for themselves. But only a precious few will look out for others."

"I understand. But how come mom didn't?"

"I think she did. But everyone has their own problems. She was more worried about you and us. And she was right to be."

"So you don't think you should have stuck up for Uncle Rob?"

"I still do. But that was the beginning of the end for your mother and I."

"How come? Did you and Uncle Rob struggle?"

"No, pal. The opposite actually. Things took off for us. The problem was, we didn't have much help, so we had to do everything ourselves. And since your Uncle Rob wasn't much of a people person, I was the one who usually had to make the deals and sign the clients. It meant I was doing quite a bit of traveling."

"I remember you being gone a lot," Josh remarked.

"Then one day, a friend of a friend introduced me to the owner of the Dodgers."

"The Los Angeles Dodgers?"

"That's right. And they wanted us to represent them in a couple of non-compete lawsuits because we had some success in that area previously. But it meant I had to live in L.A. for a while."

"Why didn't you just bring us with you?"

"I tried to..."

~

"California?!" Jane screamed.

"That's where the Dodgers play, babe."

"What's the big deal with the Dodgers?!"

"They're only one of the top sports franchises of all time. It will mean hundreds of thousands of dollars for our firm."

"But why do you have to go? Why can't TP go?"

"Because I'm the face of the firm, you know that. And when a company hires us, they expect me to be involved—at least at first. Eventually, I can turn it over to someone else, but that will take time."

"How much time?"

"Six months. A year. Maybe two."

"Two years?? What are Josh and I supposed to do?"

"I was kind of hoping you'd come with me."

"To Los Angeles?! Are you crazy?!"

"Why not? It's beautiful out there. Sunny. Warm."

"I can give you five reasons why not. Earthquakes. Floods. Landslides. Fires. Riots."

"Don't all the natural disasters count as one?"

"Don't push my buttons, Nick. I'm not in the

mood."

"Ok, but other than the reasons you mentioned, it's great."

"Plus we're not pulling Josh out of his school with his friends.

"He's *seven*. Not 17. Don't act like we'd be pulling him out of Harvard."

"What about our families?"

"What about them?"

"They all live here."

"My family's not like yours. They don't have to have a party every time someone has a bowel movement."

"Very funny."

"I'm just saying they're ok with seeing me two or three times a year."

"Well, mine's not."

Nick winked. "I'm ok with seeing yours two to three times a year."

"I'm serious. We are not going to California."

"Well, maybe WE aren't, but I have to. I'll have to commute home on the weekends."

"That won't last."

"What do you mean?"

"It won't be long before you have to work on the weekends as well. Eventually, you'll be missing birthdays and holidays."

"That will never happen."

~

Both Nick and Josh look sad at the recollection.

"She was right. It did happen. I let it happen."

"I know," Josh responded sadly. "You missed

my 8th birthday. But you did get me a really cool remote control car."

"You liked that, huh?" Nick smiled.

"Yes. But I would have rather had you there."

XI
THE DECISIONS WE MAKE~

*T*he song on the music box changed over to Joni Mitchell's *"A Case of You"* and the room blurred.

When Josh regained focus, he found himself looking at the house where his mother and he now lived. But it was two years ago. His father was in the room as well and was in the middle of an argument with her. It could have been an extension of the same argument they had three years earlier, and witnessing it again now caused all the old memories and accompanying pain that went with it to come flooding back to him.

"You haven't delivered anything you promised," Jane said in a steadfast voice. "You said a maximum of two years. It's been three. If you make it home two weekends a month, that's a lot. You've missed birthdays. School plays. Boy Scout trips."

"I know I have. And I'm sorry," Nick answered. "The transition hasn't gone as quickly as I had hoped. But I'm almost ready to turn it over to TP".

"Don't you miss your family?" she asked.

"What kind of question is that? Of course I do."

"Then come home. Permanently."

"I can't do that right now. We're in the middle of a huge copyright infringement case. If we win, we'll be set for life."

"And then what?"

"And then I'll come home."

"No, you won't. They'll always be another big case. You're missing your son growing up."

"Do you think I like being away? I'm doing this for him. I'm doing this for all of us."

"He doesn't see it that way."

"He'll appreciate it when he graduates from college without $150,000 worth of student loans to pay back."

"He's 10. He just wants you to coach his little league team."

"I'll make it up to him."

Jane sensed that in this ever-circling conversation, there would be no winner. Only losers.

"Nick, either you come home now..."

"Or?"

"Or I'm leaving you. I'm tired of feeling like the only widow whose husband is still alive."

"That's ridiculous."

"Is it? Other families go on vacation together. Our vacation is a trip to Los Angeles in order to see each other. Other families go to church together, visit relatives together, spend holidays together."

"We spend holidays together."

"You missed Christmas last year!"

Josh sat at the top of the staircase taking it all in, but he didn't really understand it. He loved his dad, but how come his dad didn't want to be with him?

~

With tears welling up in his eyes, Josh finally mustered the courage to ask what had been on his mind for the past five years. "Did you ever...did you ever think about me?"

"Of course I did, pal. That's why I wrote you nearly every day. Some days, I would leave work at lunch and go all the way home just to see if you had written me back."

"You did?" The answer seemed to make him feel a little better.

"Yes."

"Then why didn't you come home?"

Nick was very measured in his response. He had certainly had plenty of time to think about it. "The human mind is funny. Sometimes you convince yourself you're doing the right thing even when you're not."

"But how could leaving your family be the right thing?"

"I actually did come home. I was just too late. I flew back to California the day after your mom and I argued, and she filed for divorce that afternoon. Not that I blamed her. A couple of months later, I was looking out the window of my office on a typical sunny, warm California day, and I realized that everything felt wrong. It was December. There should have been snow on the ground. And I should have been with my family. So I flew home. But when I got home, I pulled into the driveway, and through the window, I saw you, your mom and some guy I didn't recognize, laughing, smiling and having dinner. And I thought that just maybe, you guys were better off without me. So I went back to California."

"The guy was Ed."

"Who was Ed?"

"Just some guy mom was introduced to. He was nice enough. But he wasn't you. And mom didn't love him."

"How do you know that?

"Because I heard her telling Aunt Cheryl one night when they thought I was sleeping. She said she couldn't date anyone when she still had "unresolved feelings" for you. Whatever that means."

"It means I screwed up. I didn't follow the most important life lesson. Family first, last and in between. I'm so sorry, pal. I guess I always thought I'd have plenty of time to make it up to you both later. Unfortunately, it doesn't look like that's going to happen exactly the way I had hoped."

Josh looked up at his father and for the first time, didn't see someone who was larger than life. Nick saw it and hated himself. But he felt powerless to do anything about it.

XII
THE RALLY~

*J*ane could hardly believe the voice on the other end of the phone at 6:30 in the morning was Nick's. It was lively, full of energy, charismatic.

"I have a favor to ask," he said. "Pull Josh out of school and take the day off of work."

"What? Are you ok?"

"I feel as good as I've felt since getting sick. I need to get out of the house, and I want you both to go with me. I have a special day planned."

"I don't know, Nick..."

"You can't see me because we're on the phone, but I'm down on my knees. Literally begging."

Jane laughed in spite of herself. "Where would we hypothetically be going?"

"That's a secret, but you'll like it. Or you'll appreciate the effort at least."

"That sounds a little suspect," she said.

"C'mon. You're not going to give a dying man his final wish? Don't ever go to work at the Make-a-Wish-Foundation, because you'd stink at it."

"Ok," she agreed at last.

He could feel her smiling through the other end of the phone.

~

"Where are we going?" Josh asked as they pulled into Nick's driveway.

"I would tell you if I knew," Jane answered as she rang the bell.

She was floored when Nick answered the door. A little thinner, but the color had returned to his face along with his winning smile. Less than 24 hours earlier he had been bed ridden, unable to stand or eat. Today he was comfortably dressed in Chinos, a navy polo, and sandals with a Notre Dame baseball cap. It was nothing short of a miracle.

She looked at Dan for some sort of explanation, but he didn't have one.

"Let's go," Nick said. "The car's here."

"The car?"

"Yeah. I got a limo. Partly because every boy should ride in a limo at least once in their life. Partly because although I feel great, I don't want to push my luck. And partly because there is no way I want to subject myself to your driving in New York City."

"Very funny," she said.

"I wasn't joking," Nick said as he winked at his son.

Josh played with every gadget in the limo as they made their way up the West Side Highway into midtown. Windows. Privacy glass. Radio. DVD player. He stood with his head through the sun roof with the wind whipping through his hair. It was every 12 year old boy's dream.

"So I should probably explain where we are

going for lunch," Nick said.

"Explain?"

"You've been here before," Nick told her.

"Did I like it?" she asked.

"Not as much as the company," he smiled.

As they turned down 52nd Street, Jane realized where they were headed. "Our diner??!"

"Yes, well, it's not a diner anymore. But it is a restaurant."

"What kind of food?"

"Alaskan."

"What?!!" both Jane and Josh screamed almost in unison.

"Relax," Nick laughed. "It's not the food, it's the company that's important."

"The company isn't *that* important," Jane remarked.

Josh liked seeing that side of his mother. Laughing. Joking. Smiling.

Nick held open the door and the hostess inside seated them right away. They were expecting them.

"So the food may be different, but they kept one thing," Nick said, pointing to the jukebox in the corner.

"Our jukebox," Jane smiled.

Nick fed a few quarters into it and flipped through some songs before settling on the one he was looking for. He walked slowly back to the table and held his hand out for Jane to dance with him as the first few guitar chords of *"Something in the Way She Moves"* began to play.

It was difficult to tell who was happiest—Nick,

Jane or Josh. Jane's hands were barely touching Nick when the song began, but by the end of it, had slid halfway down his back and were firmly gripping the sides of his shirt. When Nick spun her followed by a dip to end the song, Jane blushed a crimson shade of red.

They tried to order the least unappealing food on the menu, but when a salmon arrived at the table looking like it might swim away to find Nemo, Nick suggested they find the nearest hot dog vendor.

They stopped on their way back to Connecticut at a miniature golf course. It was old school. Not the modern courses of present day where they were just smaller versions of real golf courses. This place was miniature golf at its finest. Windmill. Clown's mouth. Ramps. Bump boards. Its character was also probably the main reason it was crowded on a Wednesday night.

"Tell you what. You and your mom play as a team. We will count whoever has the lowest score between the two of you for each hole."

"Big deal," Jane said. "If you're better than both of us, how is that going to help?"

"I might be better than you, but not necessarily on every hole. You guys have two chances each hole to beat me."

"We got this, mom."

"Because I'm feeling generous, I'll even throw in another wrinkle. You can tell me how I have to play each hole. Left-handed. Between the legs. Behind my back. Whatever you want."

Does his best Chevy Chase Caddyshack

impression.   Yaahtaaatatata.   Nannananana.
Yaahtaaatatata.

"You're on," Josh said.

Nick sunk a hole in one left handed on the first hole. Josh had him putt between his legs for the 2nd hole. Then behind his back. On one leg. Pool cue style. With the club reversed. The club upside down. Seventeen holes later he sat with a score of 23 and a crowd had started to assemble. For the final hole, Nick putted blindfolded, using Jane's hairband to cover his eyes, with one arm, sideways, between his legs. After hitting the ball, he leaned in with his hand cupped around his ear and listened for the "plunk" of the ball in the cup. The place erupted when it dropped.

"Now you're just showing off," Jane smirked, shaking her head.

"It's not showing off when you can't help yourself," Nick answered.

Ice cream was a must on the way home. Josh devoured a waffle cone of mint chocolate chip with sprinkles in seconds flat. Jane went for the more traditional soft vanilla chocolate swirl. Nick had slowed a bit by this time, the events of the day having sapped him of most of his energy, but he was enjoying himself nonetheless.

"I feel badly, dad," Josh said. "We went to the place of your and mom's first date for her. We went miniature golfing and got ice cream for me. But we didn't do anything you wanted to do."

"Are you kidding? Everything we did exactly what I wanted to do, because it was with you guys."

Josh was asleep about ten seconds after he climbed back in the limo. He looked so peaceful.

"Thank you for bringing him today," Nick said.

"He wanted to see you."

"And thank you for taking him to get the music box. It's the best present I've ever gotten."

"Then you need to make some better friends. That was a Big Al's special."

"I don't know what you paid for it, but it was worth every penny. And the songs he put on the tape were top notch. I can't believe he remembered the songs I told him about."

"He remembers every thing you tell him."

Nick squirmed a little. There was more that he wanted to say. He just wasn't sure how to say it.

"I know this is a little late. Actually it's a lotta late. But I wanted to say I'm sorry," he finally blurted.

"For what?" Jane asked, knowing full well what he was referring to.

"For everything. For screwing up our family for starters. I honestly thought I was doing what was best for us in the long run. Figured if I worked hard and made a ton of money, we'd be set and I could spend the rest of our lives making it up to you both."

"I never needed a lot of money. I would have rather had you around."

"I know. I messed up. Ironically, if I hadn't gone to California, we would have spent more time together, but you'd be in tough shape financially— especially given the circumstances."

"What circumstances?"

"Me dying."

"You're going to outlive us all. You're on the road to recovery," she said.

"Not to be too much of a downer, but it's the end of the road for me. They let me come home because there isn't much else they can do."

"But what about today? You seem so much better! Has it been an act?"

"Can't really explain today. Just woke up feeling much better."

"Maybe the doctors are wrong?"

"Maybe," he said. "But in case they're not..."

He pulled a bound set of papers from the pocket on the door.

"What's this?"

"Read it."

She began flipping through it. Realized what it was.

"I don't want to read your will, Nick."

"Why not? I'm leaving everything to you, Josh and Dan."

"Josh and Dan I understand. But me?"

"You're the only woman I've ever loved. I knew it from the moment I first looked into your eyes at the diner."

Jane smiled shyly. "I didn't think you thought about those things anymore."

"Are you kidding? I think about them all the time."

She leaned over and kissed him. Softly. Lovingly.

"Does that mean you forgive me?"

"Yes, I forgive you. But if you live, I reserve

the right to make you pay for it for a number of years."

"I've got one more favor to ask of you," Nick said.

"What is it?"

"I'd like to see you both as often as you can come by, but when things get really bad, I don't want Josh to be here. I don't want his last memories of me to be awful ones."

"I have a feeling his last memories of you are going to be some of his best," she smiled.

XIII
REQUIEM ~

The call came early the next morning. Dan explained that doctors described Nick's dramatic improvement of less than twelve hours earlier as what was referred to as a "Rally"; when a terminally ill patient's condition drastically improves without explanation, days, or in this instance, hours, before passing away. Although there was no medical evidence to support it, they believed it was the human spirit's desire to wrap up any loose ends in their life before moving on. Once Nick had done that he was able to let go, and finally have a peaceful night's sleep that would last for eternity.

Josh could hear his mother's muffled sobs from upstairs. "It's dad, isn't it?" he yelled down.

When she couldn't answer him over her uncontrolled sobbing, he quietly walked downstairs and placed his hand on her shoulder. "Did I make him more sick by having him out so late yesterday?" he asked.

Jane immediately went into mother mode, which is to say that she put her own grief on hold so she could comfort her son. "No, baby. You were the reason he lasted as long as he did."

She hugged him close with the intention of not letting him go until he turned at least 18, thinking that if she held on tight enough, she could freeze time.

The wake was two days later, and the line outside the funeral home was four wide and wrapped around the building three times. Wakes were difficult. Trying to comfort people who were trying to comfort you usually only led to more tears. Making small talk with people you hadn't seen in years and likely would never see again was awkward. But Josh, his mother and Dan stood and greeted each and every person that came. It took nearly five hours to do so. Once the last person had come through, Josh noticed an older man, had to be close to 80, seated in a chair at the front of the room. He had actually seen him walk in at the very beginning, but the man never came through the line. Never said a word. And apparently, never left. He finally rose to his feet, steadied himself, and made his way over to Josh.

"I didn't know your father well," he began, "but I liked him very much. I was a janitor in his office building a few years ago. Every morning he'd say hello to me and bring me a coffee. At Christmas, he'd give me a card and some money. He was the only person in the entire building that ever did. About six months ago, my wife passed away. I hadn't seen your dad in quite some time. I heard he changed jobs. But out of the blue, he showed up at my wife's wake. At first, we just made small talk. And then I introduced him to some of my wife and my friends. Before I knew it, four hours had passed and he was still there—right next to me. I felt badly and told him he didn't need to stay all that time and he looked at me and said, '*You have always been a friendly, hard working, chivalrous man in a world where that is a rarity. When I saw your wife had passed, that you had no kids, and that you had outlived all of your relatives as well, there was no way I was going to let a person like you go through something like this alone.*'"

Tears welled up into small pools in Josh's eyes. His mother covered most of her face in an effort to prevent herself from breaking down again. Dan smiled a sad smile as this man confirmed something he already knew about his brother.

"I just thought you should know what a terrific person your father was," the man said.

Josh, not one prone to displays of affection, reached out and hugged the gentleman, and suddenly felt as close to his father as he ever had.

The funeral was the following morning and every seat in the church was filled. Josh had asked his mother to speak, and made his way to the podium amidst the quiet shuffling of paper programs and muffled sniffles. He was smartly dressed in a navy suit, pressed white shirt, and a red tie. Reaching into a side pocket on his suit coat, he removed a handwritten note. He didn't really mind speaking in public. Just like anyone else, he would get butterflies in the pit of his stomach, but as soon as he focused on the one person in the audience he knew would smile at him and provide comfort—in this instance it was his mother—he was fine.

"I've always loved and respected my father for everything he stood for, but it wasn't until recently that I really got to know him," Josh began. "My father taught me 12 life lessons to live by. He said there were 12 because it was his 2nd favorite number and 17 was too many. He also made sure I wrote them down so I wouldn't forget them because he said they were '*gems*'."

There were smiles and chuckles in the audience.

"I wanted to share them with you today so you could hopefully all get to know my dad better too. If you don't understand them, don't feel badly, because I didn't either at first. But I think I do now. Number 1. Be honest. You can have no honor without honesty. Number 2. The only time it's ok to be dishonest, is if you're trying to help someone and doing the honest thing would cost you a lot of money."

Laughter spread through the room.

"Number 3. When a once in a lifetime opportunity comes along, make that a priority. Number 4. Spend time doing things you don't want to do, because by the time you *want* to do them, it will be too late. Number 5. Don't kiss fat girls. But if you do, make sure there are no witnesses."

Full out laughter. Jane shook her head and rolled her eyes. It sounded like something Nick would say.

"Number 6. Have a sense of humor. It's the

most valuable thing you can ever have for free. Number 7. Knowing you've met the right girl is like an Italian knowing when the spaghetti is done. You just know. Number 8. Give people the benefit of the doubt. Usually they'll end up disappointing you, but every once in a while they'll surprise you and that's what makes life worth living. Number 9. Be loyal to your friends. Any—," he stopped himself just short of using the word *asshole*, which he had written on the paper, "Any *jerk* can look out for themselves. Number 10. Everyone makes mistakes. You won't appreciate the good times unless you've eaten a little--," looked down, saw the word *shit*, made another change on the fly, "*crap* every now and then. Number 11. Don't be afraid to say you're sorry. No person has ever been disappointed to get an apology. And finally, Number 12. Family first, last and in between."

Josh paused, breathed a sigh of relief that he had made it through, and smiled at his mother. "Thank you very much for coming today. My dad would have appreciated it."

~

"Wow. It's really late," Josh said to his son, after checking his watch. The story had taken up the better part of two hours. "You need to get some sleep, young man."

"I'm not tired," Timmy answered. "I really do wish I could have known your dad."

"Me too, pal."

"But I feel like I know him a little bit now. Thanks."

"Maybe there's a way for you to get to know him even better. I was going to wait until your birthday to give this to you, but a little early present couldn't hurt..."

Josh reached under the bed and pulled out a wrapped package. Handed it to his son.

"You hid my present under *my* bed?"

"Figured it was the one place you wouldn't look. Besides, with your mess, you'd never find it there."

"Is this???" Timmy asked excitedly.

"Open it," Josh smiled.

Tim tore off the wrapping paper and found the music box inside.

"I had an electronics place make a slight alteration to it since tape decks are kind of out of date. They connected an IPod to it," Josh explained.

"Oh my god, dad, this is awesome! It is really the best present ever. Does it work?"

"Of course it works."

"No, I mean, does it *work*?"

"Only one way to find that out. But not now. It's bedtime."

He reached over and turned off the light. Ruffled Timmy's hair.

"Dad?"

"Yeah, pal?"

"You're a lot like your dad, ya know. Only even better."

"Thanks, pal," he said, tearing up. "Goodnight."

Josh found his wife standing outside the room as he left.

"How long have you been here?" he asked.

"Long enough. How come you never told me that story?"

"I guess that would be because some stories are meant to be shared only between a father and son."

"And what happens when he finds out the box doesn't really work?"

"Oh, it works," Josh winked. "Believe me, it works."

XIV
SUNDAYS AGAIN

*T*wo weeks passed uneventfully, after Josh had relayed the story of the music box to his son. Then one Sunday morning he went to check on Tim to see if he was ready to leave for his soccer game.

"Do you think it would be ok if I missed my game today and went to see grandma instead?" Timmy asked.

"You not feeling well?" Josh asked.

Normally it would have taken an army of storm troopers to drag him away from a game.

"I feel ok. Just wanted to see grandma."

~

There was a bit of rustling inside the house, before Jane opened the front door. "I'm surprised to see you guys," she said. "I thought you had a soccer game today."

"I did," Timmy answered, "but I wanted to see you instead."

She was taken aback, in a good way, and stepped aside to let them enter. Josh poured some soft drinks in the kitchen and returned to the living room to see Timmy with his hand extended for his grandmother to take.

"What's this all about?" Jane asked.

"It's a Reynold's men tradition," Timmy answered proudly.

Jane knew the song from the moment she heard the first chord come out of the music box, and she had listened to Nick's father tell the story about Nick dancing with his grandmother to Frank Sinatra enough times that she felt like she had been there herself. She took Timmy's hand and began dancing with him. They were soon joined by Josh and Colleen. They all danced. And smiled. And laughed. But they didn't drink prune juice or eat tapioca pudding.

Timmy changed his clothes quickly after they returned home, and waved goodbye to his parents.

"Where are you off to?" Josh asked.

"Just going to Steve's house."

"Ok then. Well, don't be too late."

"I won't," Timmy promised.

Fifteen minutes later, Timmy rode into a cemetery lot and leaned his bike against a tree. He began searching the headstones until he found the one he was looking for. *"Nick Reynolds 1949-1991 Honesty, Loyalty, Family"*.

"Hi Grandpa," Timmy said as he stood over the grave, "We've never met, but I feel like I know you."

He reached into his backpack and removed the music box, placing it gently in front of the grave.

"My dad gave this to you on his 12th birthday.

And he gave it to me for mine a few weeks ago. This song is the first song he and my mother ever danced to. Anyway, I thought maybe you'd like to see how he turned out," he said, and then added, "He turned out great by the way."

Timmy pushed the button on the IPod and the Counting Crows *"Mrs. Potter's Lullaby"* began to play.

A few rows over at that moment, a car was parked next to a large oak tree. Josh and Jane stood next to it. Timmy couldn't see them from where he was.

"This is the first song Colleen and I ever danced to," Josh said to his mother. "But you've probably never heard it since you are kind of old."

"I know who the Counting Crows are, smart guy. Of all the qualities you could have gotten from your father, you had to get his sense of humor."

"You say that like it's a bad thing," Josh smirked.

"Well..." his mother responded. "So how did you know he was going to be here today?"

"Just a hunch. He asked me for a list of my favorite songs last night."

"And what happens when he finds out the music box doesn't really work?"

"Does it look like it doesn't work?" Josh asked.

They looked over at Timmy while he lay on the ground with his arms folded neatly behind his head, a smile on his face that stretched from ear to ear.

"I'm afraid I just don't see anything," Jane remarked sadly.

"Well, some things are only meant to be shared between a father and son," Josh answered before adding, "but other things...can be seen if you really believe in them."

Jane gave him a frustrated glance as she leaned against the tree, music still flowing in the not so far off distance. She stared at the multicolored leaves on the trees with the crystal clear blue sky in the background, and all the beautiful colors slowly melded into one brilliant canvas. Within it, she saw the outline of a familiar, well-chiseled, shadowy figure that became clearer with every moment. Was it the magic of the music box? The sway of the music itself? Or the sheer power of the human mind at work? Did it really matter? The familiar face stepped forward from the shadows, and she smiled at him.

The way all women did.

Author's Notes

The character of Nick Reynolds is like my father was in many ways, but completely unlike him in many others. Quite simply, my father was the greatest person I've ever known. He didn't invent a cure for Cancer, or run for President. He wasn't a neurosurgeon who saved hundreds of lives. He wasn't a billionaire. He was just a smart, funny, honest, decent family man in a world that could desperately use more of them. He was home for dinner with the family each and every night. He never missed an event my sister or I participated in. And he treated my mother with love and respect. My dad has been gone for a few years now, but a day rarely passes where I don't think about him in some manner. Where I don't wonder what he would say in a certain situation. If he would be proud of the man I've become. I strive each day to be more like him, knowing that I will probably never quite achieve it, but the thought of him encourages me to relentlessly pursue it nonetheless. This story is for him.

Enjoy this book? Turn the page for a preview of another of my books, the romantic comedy, ***Nick Nelson Was Here***...

NICK NELSON WAS HERE

"There is only one kind of love, but there are a thousand imitations."

La Rochefoucauld

I
THE LAST OF THE NICE GUYS

*N*ick Nelson was first brandished with the moniker "the last of the nice guys" after leaving a pickup basketball game in 6th grade to help an elderly lady he didn't know, carry her groceries 17 blocks to her house. He did little to change that view of him when he went to his Senior Prom with a girl in a wheelchair, and he cemented it forevermore after driving his roommate's one night stand home *for* him, when his roommate got called into work. He even bought her breakfast on the way.

The label was something he was neither proud of, nor abhorred, for he knew the title and a quarter would only get him a phone call at a pay phone. But it was also his even keeled personality that enabled him to brush off days that would have driven a lessor person wild.

~

The line at the tax office was ten deep as it usually was at the end of the month. An array of people of varying ages and economic stature waited; some patiently, others, not so much.

"I'm here to pay my son's car tax," an elderly

woman announced to no one in particular. She was a kindly looking woman, well-dressed, with curly white hair and soft skin.

"Is he in high school?" another woman asked, the slight tilt of her head indicating that she wondered how a woman in her seventies could have a teenage son.

"Oh, no," the elderly woman responded. "He's 41, but he lives at home with us. So does his brother who's 47."

"Neither of them is married?"

"They've never been. They have it pretty good. We don't make them pay rent, and I cook for them. They have plenty of money to spend as they choose."

An older man entered the conversation at that point. His tightly cropped hair and posture that was much straighter than normal for someone his age, led Nick to believe he might be a veteran.

"Smart boys. A little ice cream ain't worth 40 years of misery," he said.

Nick, silent until that point, spit the water he was sipping across the floor. Nick Nelson was average in nearly every manner used to describe a person physically except for one. He had abnormally large feet. He credited that feature for the first of his two self-proclaimed talents—his ability to fall asleep anywhere, at any time--even while standing up; and his ability to listen in on other people's conversations without making it seem as though he was. Although spitting the water onto the linoleum tiles of the tax office left some question about his second talent.

"I don't think I'd ever get married again," the second woman said, as if she was hoping Nick would try to talk her out of it.

"No?" Nick asked politely. The woman had probably been pretty at one time, but life seemed to have worn her down. She wasn't particularly heavy, yet not tone either, and her tan skin had a sort of leatherette look to it, as if it needed to be sanded down first before color was applied. She was probably in her late-thirties, but appeared much older. The fact that she was there in the middle of the day and the fact that her tan was much darker than a two-day weekend tan, told him that she worked nights, most likely at a grocery store or something of that nature.

"What about you? Have you ever been married?" she asked.

"Not yet. Still fighting the good fight."

The crusty vet winked and nodded his approval, while his wife, having recently joined him in line, slapped him across the arm, causing him to roll his eyes.

"I'm not opposed to it," Nick added almost as an afterthought. "But she would have to be a pretty special woman."

"Don't say a word!" the vet's wife responded before her husband could.

The conversation was interrupted by the screaming of a two year old boy, whose three year old brother had just pushed him over. When his young mother reprimanded him, the three year old began to pound his forehead off the floor.

"Matthew! No!" she shouted desperately as

she tried to pull him from the floor.

"My parents told me I used to bang my head on the floor when I was little," Nick offered.

"I'm worried he's going to hurt himself," she answered as he wriggled free from her grasp.

"Well, I wouldn't encourage it," Nick said with a smile, "but I turned out ok."

"Next," the woman at window 2 said, her eyes widening to indicate she was ready for Nick.

"How are you?" he said as he approached.

"How can I help you?" she answered in a tone that expressed she had little desire to do exactly that.

"I'm just looking to pick up a couple of beach parking stickers."

"Do you have your license and registration with you?"

"My license, yes. I didn't think I needed my registration."

"I should be able to pull it up on the computer. What's the plate number?"

"I have two cars actually, and ummm....neither have personalized plates, so I don't really know the plate numbers to be honest."

"What's your address?" the woman droned.

"Same as on my driver's license," Nick answered with a smile.

She punched in a few keys, then stared blankly at the screen for a moment or two. "I don't have any cars registered to you in Stamford," she said at last.

"I have two of them. One's parked out front," Nick reassured her.

"I see a blue Hummer registered to you in Fairfield."

"That's where I used to live."

"Did you ever transfer over the registration?"

His lack of a response told her the answer was no.

"I didn't know I had to," he answered at last. "But the other car should definitely be in there. I bought it long after I moved. I've only had it for two months."

"Well, that's why it's not showing up in the system then. They update it every six months. You said you have that car with you?"

"Yes. It's out front."

"Can you go get the registration?"

Nick looked at her and then at the ever-growing line that had now spilled out into the corridor.

"I'll give you a pass to come right to the window," she said in the tone of an irritated high school teacher.

"Thank you," he said as he took the pass. "I'll be right back."

When he returned, the young woman with the two young boys was still a good five people away from the window. She seemed to be at her last wit. Nick took a deep breath and handed her his pass as if it was the golden ticket to get into the Chocolate Factory. She took it gratefully. The woman at the window scowled at Nick. The passes were supposed to be non-transferable, but she was tired of listening to the boy pound his head off the floor as well, so she let it slide.

Thirty minutes later, Nick was finally at the window again. He handed her his registration, which she studied carefully.

"This is a temporary registration," she said.

"It's what they gave me," Nick explained.

"It's expired."

"I haven't received a permanent one yet."

"I can't accept this."

"Are you serious?"

"Yes, I'm serious. You have one car whose registration has expired and another not even registered in town."

"My driver's license is up to date and I promise you both cars made the trip to Stamford with me. I didn't leave them behind."

"You live on Beach Avenue. Why do you even need beach stickers anyway?' the woman asked.

"Well, that's actually kind of a long story," Nick began. "You see, a few weeks ago, I had my roof redone, and the guys doing it used a big tree I had in the yard as a scaffold to work on certain areas of the roof. Anyway, about a week later, in the middle of the night, I heard this huge crash, and looked out the window to see that the tree had fallen into the street. Well, the Public Works guys didn't chop the tree up for me. They simply picked it up and tossed it back into my yard. So, I then had to hire someone to come out, chop the tree up and grind up the stump. While they were doing that, their huge wood-chipper truck, chipped my driveway. That chip soon became a sinkhole. So, I had to get an engineer out and he said I needed to get it repaired as soon as possible and he recommended having the entire driveway redone. They're doing that as we speak, but I won't be able to drive on it for a couple of days, so I have to park my cars in the lot down the street. I wanted the beach stickers so I could park there without getting a bunch of parking tickets."

Most people, after hearing a story like that, would have relented and handed over the stickers. "Sorry I'm afraid I can't help you," the woman answered before turning to the next person in line. "Next."

At that point, some people would have responded with a string of expletives and thrown something. Nick merely nodded his head as if her response made sense and walked silently from the office.

He took a deep breath once outside. He loved the smells and sounds of late summer. Freshly cut grass. Flowers on their second bloom. The tide rolling in. He opened the passenger door of his car and placed his expired, temporary registration certificate inside the glove compartment before walking around to the other side. On the windshield was a canary yellow parking ticket. He had exceeded the 60 minute allotment. Many people at this point would have torn the ticket to bits and left the pieces on the street. Nick tossed it onto his passenger seat.

"Nice car," a voice said from behind him.

He looked up and saw the woman with the leatherette skin from the tax office waiting at the bus stop. "Thanks," he answered. "I just got it a couple of months ago."

"A Porsche, right?"

"Yes," he answered, almost embarrassedly.

"You can definitely tell you're not married," the woman laughed.

"Yeah, I figured I'd have my mid-life crisis a little early. You need a ride?" Nick asked.

"I don't want to put you out."

"You're not putting me out. I've got nowhere in particular to be."

"Well, I never have ridden in a Porsche," the woman said as she climbed in. "I'm Cheryl."

"Nick," he answered, formally introducing himself for the first time. "Where to, Cheryl?"

"The Super Stop & Shop over by the mall. I really appreciate this. I'm supposed to be at work by 4:30, and I think I'd be late if I had to wait for the next bus."

"No problem."

"So what do you do for a living?" she asked.

"I'm a producer for a small town Saturday morning television talk show called *Fairfield County Weekly*."

"I've heard of it, but never seen it," she said politely. He figured she had probably never even heard of it.

"Yeah, it's got kind of a small audience."

"It can't be that small if you're driving a car like this," she remarked.

"Like I said, I'm single. No wife. No kids," he laughed.

"There's Margie!" the woman exclaimed as they pulled into the parking lot. "Do you think you could do me a favor and drop me off in the front? She'll shit gold bricks if she sees me getting out of this car."

"Well, let's hope she does," Nick said. "Gold bricks are very valuable."

"You know, the Oyster Fest is this weekend," Cheryl said as she scribbled a number on the back of a business card. "If you're around, give me a call."

"Thanks. If I'm around, I will."

"Thanks again for the ride."

"You're welcome."

He flipped over the card. It was a salesman's card for office supplies. The guy must have given it to her. Now she had given it to him. It was wonder anyone ever got married. She was nice enough, but not his type. If he ever walked down the aisle, he wanted it to be with someone that was also experiencing it for the first time as well. He would toss the card in the "if I'm lonely and desperate box" in his kitchen when he got home.

The pavers were just finishing up at his house as he pulled up to the curb. He had to admit. The driveway did look nice.

"All finished?" Nick asked.

"Yeah. You can walk on it, but I wouldn't drive on it for a couple of days. And I would make sure any fat friends go in through the front door," the gruff paver responded.

"Here's your money," Nick said, handing him an envelope of cash.

"Thanks. We filled that hole pretty good and paved up a solid two inches. You should be all set now."

"Great."

Nick looked at his house as the trucks pulled
away. It had been his dream house for years, and
when it finally went on sale three years ago, he
jumped at the opportunity.

The house was a large white colonial, much
larger than needed for a single person, with
gleaming round pillars anchoring it in the front and
sliding glass doors on both levels opening to a
spectacular view of the Long Island Sound out
back. The yard was meticulously kept, with a four-
foot boxwood hedge shielding it from outsiders.
He did notice, however, that the grass was getting a
bit unruly. Nick went over to the crawlspace where
he stored his lawnmower and pulled on the door.
It wouldn't open. He pulled again, harder this
time and it opened slightly before jamming. Nick
looked down and shook his head in amazement.
The pavers had paved in his crawlspace.

At this point, most people would have
embarked on a five state killing spree. But Nick
Nelson was not most people. Instead, the last of
the nice guys merely chuckled, his chuckle soon
becoming a hearty laugh at the absurdity of it all.